WEST OF
ROCK RIVER

Also by John D. Nesbitt
in Large Print:

Black Hat Butte
For the Norden Boys
North of Cheyenne
Red Wind Crossing
Black Diamond Rendezvous
Coyote Trail
Man from Wolf River
Wild Rose of Ruby Canyon

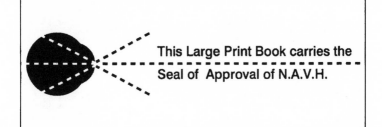

WEST OF ROCK RIVER

John D. Nesbitt

Thorndike Press • Waterville, Maine

Published in 2005 by arrangement with Leisure Books, a division of Dorchester Publishing Co., Inc.

Thorndike Press® Large Print Western.

The tree indicium is a trademark of Thorndike Press.

The text of this Large Print edition is unabridged. Other aspects of the book may vary from the original edition.

Set in 16 pt. Plantin by Minnie B. Raven.

Printed in the United States on permanent paper.

Library of Congress Cataloging-in-Publication Data

Nesbitt, John D.
    West of Rock River / by John D. Nesbitt.
        p. cm. — (Thorndike Press large print Western)
    ISBN 0-7862-7410-7 (lg. print : hc : alk. paper)
    1. Brothers — Death — Fiction.   2. Male friendship
— Fiction.   3. Revenge — Fiction.   4. Large type
books.   I. Title.   II. Thorndike Press large print
Western series.
PS3564.E76W47 2005
813'.54—dc22   2004028357

For my sister, Jackie Lee.

As the Founder/CEO of NAVH, the only national health agency solely devoted to those who, although not totally blind, have an eye disease which could lead to serious visual impairment, I am pleased to recognize Thorndike Press* as one of the leading publishers in the large print field.

Founded in 1954 in San Francisco to prepare large print textbooks for partially seeing children, NAVH became the pioneer and standard setting agency in the preparation of large type.

Today, those publishers who meet our standards carry the prestigious "Seal of Approval" indicating high quality large print. We are delighted that Thorndike Press is one of the publishers whose titles meet these standards. We are also pleased to recognize the significant contribution Thorndike Press is making in this important and growing field.

Lorraine H. Marchi, L.H.D.
Founder/CEO
NAVH

* Thorndike Press encompasses the following imprints: Thorndike, Wheeler, Walker and Large Print Press.

Chapter One

Vance Coolidge stopped his horse and leaned forward in the saddle. Two sets of tracks leading to his cabin could mean anything — fellows he knew and got along with, men he knew and didn't get along with, or strangers just passing through. It could mean one rider with a packhorse, but the tracks didn't stay even enough for one horse to be following another. Two riders, then, he thought. In some ways, that was better than one.

Vance sat up straight and took another look around at the country. The plains rolled away in every direction, paling now in the late July heat. The full green of early summer had faded to lighter tones, and the new growth of sagebrush lent a silver tint to the grassland. Nothing moved. The dots in the north would be someone's cattle other than his own. Off to the south, a couple of gashes in the land showed whitish tan like the flanks of antelope, but Vance saw the same shapes every day and knew they did not move. Straight west, with its back up against a low ridge, sat his cabin. He imagined there was some movement going on inside, but from without, it looked as lifeless as a stone.

The two sets of tracks led up to the cabin, milled around, then led off to the southwest. As Vance came within thirty yards of his hitching rail, the front door of the cabin opened and a blue shape appeared.

Josie didn't speak until Vance dismounted and walked the last few yards.

"The Dunham brothers were here."

"Which ones?"

"Fred and Tip."

"Oh." That was better than Fred and Moon, anyway. Tip was the best of the three, it seemed. As for the other two, Vance could take them or leave them.

Josie's voice came from the shadow of the doorway. "They said they'd come back later."

"Did they say what it was about?"

"No, not at all. I said I expected you in for dinner, and they said they'd drop by again."

Vance looked at Josie, his gaze roving over the blue dress as if there was something he was trying to recognize. For a couple of seconds his eyes met hers, then moved away. "Thanks," he said. "I'll put my horse away, and then I'll come in. Everything else all right?"

"Sure."

Vance nodded, and Josie went back inside. That was the way things had been, he thought — not much spark. As he led his horse around back, he wondered what the Dunham boys wanted. If one of the others as well as Tip had dropped by, and if they were coming back, they were sure to want something.

Josie didn't have much to say as she set out the meal. The stew and the biscuits were the same as she had served the evening before, but it was still good grub, and Vance had two helpings. Then his eyebrows went up as Josie uncovered a pot of rice pudding with raisins.

"Spotted puppy," he said. "Now that's good."

Josie gave a faint smile as she brought out two clean enamel bowls and served the pudding.

Vance realized things had been pretty quiet. "Is the baby asleep?"

Josie swallowed a spoonful of rice and said, "Yes, he is. He's been sleeping well, even in the warm part of the day."

"That's good."

"Uh-huh."

"You know, some cooks boil it in a cloth bag, but I can't see where it's any better that way."

"The speckled puppy."

"Yeah."

"I'm glad you like it." She brushed back her dark hair.

"Sure. It's fine," he said. His glance met hers again for a moment, and he noticed her eyes, the color of flax blossoms and summer sky.

When he was through eating he got up from the table, put on his hat, and went out the back door. He needed to find a task that would take up his time until the Dunham brothers returned. He never had any shortage of work needing to be done, but at the moment he wanted something small that wouldn't matter if it got interrupted. He went into the stable and looked around until he settled on a tangle of rope.

A small wave of irritation moved through him as he looked at the heap. A couple of weeks earlier, a Mormon had camped about a half mile away and had asked to borrow some rope to set up a corral until he could get an axle fixed. Vance lent him three ropes, and they came back all in a tangle. It happened when Vance was out checking cattle, so he didn't even get a chance to see how many wives, if any, the man had with him. All Vance got for his trouble was a bundle of knots to pick at.

Coming out of the stable, he squinted in the sunlight. There was little shade in this place, and even less at midday. He thought he might find a little on the front step, where he could keep an eye out as well. As he carried the ropes around to the front of the cabin, he reminded himself that some fellows wouldn't have bothered to return the ropes at all. Fred and Moon Dunham had been that way for as long as he had known them, dropping by to borrow a strap for saddle leather, a handful of nails, a pound of coffee. "I'll ketch ya back later" was their favorite phrase and, more often than not, later never came.

Vance picked at the knots, pushing and pulling and twisting the coarse hemp. He wondered what the Mormon had used the ropes for, to make such a mess and get the knots so tight. Whatever it was, the fellow was long gone, and he had at least given back the ropes.

The shadow of the house had reached out to cover the step, and Vance's right thumb and forefinger were starting to feel sore, when Fred and Tip Dunham came riding up at a fast walk. Vance sometimes had to look twice to know if it was Fred or Moon. Fred had light blond hair that looked almost white in the shadow of his hat, but it was a normal hue. Moon's hair, which was white enough to look unnatural, had a strange tone to it even at a distance, so Vance could tell the brothers apart. Fred was the one who didn't look so much like a ghost.

Fred was riding a big sorrel, and Tip rode alongside on a chestnut. Any time a fellow saw two or all three of the Dunhams, Tip was easiest to pick out. The youngest of the brothers, he had the lightest build and the thinnest features, and his hair was a little darker, somewhere between blond and brown. Today his face was in shadow, like his brother's, so Vance could not get an impression until the two riders slowed to a stop.

Then he saw that they both had trouble marked on them.

"Hullo, boys," he said. "What's up?"

Fred's voice came out tense. "Came by earlier."

"That's what Josie said." Vance looked at Tip, who just winced.

Fred didn't say anything as he swung down from the saddle. Vance recognized the air that Fred liked to carry at moments such as this, when he left the other person waiting for an answer as he made his physical presence felt. Fred was a husky man with thick features, and he had learned to draw himself up square and loom over others. He did so now with a pained expression on his face.

Vance set the tangled rope aside as he stood up. He looked at Fred, then at Tip, then back at Fred. "Well?"

Fred's yellow teeth showed as he spoke. "Bad." Then after a few seconds he said, "Moon's been killed."

Vance felt a shock ripple through his upper body. "Killed?"

"That's right."

Vance shook his head and glanced at Tip, whose face was clouded and who still didn't speak. Looking back at Fred, he asked, "How?"

Fred took a deep breath and tipped his head back, flaring his nostrils and shaking his head. "Couple of sons of bitches."

"Was he by himself?"

"Far as I know."

"Who were the killers? Anyone I know?"

"Fellow named Rusk and a Mexican pal of his."

Vance stared at the ground and shook his head. The name meant nothing to him.

All he could picture was Moon the tow-head, off a ways and silent. Here were the two brothers, alive and anguished, while Moon was on his back somewhere, with his eyes closed for good. Vance looked up at Fred. "Rusk, huh? Never heard of him. How sure are you?"

"Damn sure. He'd been hangin' around town for a day, and more than one person got his name. Seems he knew Marianne, maybe too well for anyone's good. Him and Moon had words right there in town."

"When was that?"

"Last night."

"What was Moon doing in town?"

Fred took another breath. "As I understand it, Marianne went to town and took a room, and Moon went to bring her back."

"And this fellow Rusk got in the middle of it?"

"That's right. Him and the Mexican jumped Moon out on the edge of town later last night, and then they rode like hell."

"Which way?"

"West."

"Uh-huh." Vance looked at Fred's face. It carried a dull shine of sweat that gave the features a waxy texture. "What was

Moon doing on the edge of town?"

"I guess they called him out."

Vance frowned. It didn't sound as if the other two had actually jumped him, then, but it was a small point to argue with a man whose brother had just been killed. "So where's Marianne, then? Still in town?"

"They say she went back out to the place."

Vance looked at Tip and then back at Fred. "So what are you fellas plannin' to do?"

"Go after the sons of bitches." Fred lifted his chin, as if he were putting his grief on exhibit. "By the time the law gets around to doin' anything, these bastards'll be long gone. They've got half a day's start on us, and I think we can catch 'em."

"I see." If the brothers had come by twice rather than taking out right away, it wasn't just to give the news. They were in a hurry, but they didn't want to go alone.

Fred's voice came back with authority. "Moon was our brother."

"I know."

"And you can't sit around and wait for someone to send word down to Laramie, over to Rawlins, and then send a telegram to Cheyenne, and all that. If they'd robbed a train or pulled a bank job, there'd be a posse out there right now. But no one cares about Moon Dunham — that is, no one who should be doing something. If he had more money, or if these sons of bitches had stolen some money from someone who did, things would be different. But they aren't. And we're not gonna wait around and watch the law drag its ass until it's too late. We know who did it, and we know which way they went."

Vance shrugged. Fred had a way of sounding as if he were the only one who could be right, but Vance still felt sympathy for him. He and Tip had lost a brother. "I can't blame you," he said.

Fred brought out a bag of Bull Durham, troughed a paper, and shook out some tobacco. He didn't speak until he had rolled the cigarette, licked and tapped the seam, and, chest out, lit the cigarette. "We're askin' for help," he said as he blew away the smoke.

"You want me to go along, I take it."

Fred took another drag and blew the smoke out through his nostrils. "We could use the help. There's two of them, and they may be hard to handle."

Vance looked at Tip, whose face had opened up, and then back at Fred. "How many do you want to go with?"

"Four. The two of us, and two more. We came to you first, Vance. We know you're a good hand, and you've always been a friend to all three of us."

Vance had an image of Moon again — Moon the sunhead, off in the background. "Who's taking care of things in town?"

"What things?"

"You know — arrangements."

Fred sniffed. "I left word for Marianne to take care of that. I said we'd be gone three, maybe four days at the most. If we don't catch 'em by then, we'll say to hell with it and come back for the funeral. At least we tried."

Vance raised his eyebrows and looked at the ground.

"I know it seems like a lot to ask," Fred went on. "But it'll just be for a few days. Mainly what we're askin' for is someone to back us up, to give us a little more weight."

Vance lifted his head. "I'm like everyone else. I couldn't stay gone long, even if I wanted. I've got a place to look after, cattle to keep an eye on. And a wife. And a little baby."

Fred squinted and nodded as he took a drag on his cigarette. "We know that. But we're askin' you as a friend of ours, and as a friend of Moon's."

The last part didn't add much to Fred's persuasive effect. Vance didn't think Moon had ever been that special a friend — not like Tip, for example. Vance looked at the youngest brother.

"What do you say, Tip? You haven't said anything so far."

"I don't know what else there is to say. Like Fred already said, Moon was our brother. And you're our friend. We were hopin' to count on you."

"Uh-huh."

"And it just seems to us that a man who's been done wrong should have a chance to get even."

Vance wasn't sure what Tip meant — whether the party who had been done wrong was Moon or the two brothers who were still alive. But the simpleness of the statement did more toward convincing him than anything Fred had said so far. "I'd have to agree with that," he said. Then he turned to Fred again. "You say four days at the most?"

Fred gave a quick up-and-down shake to his head. "We can't stay gone that long ourselves. We should be able to do something in that time, and if not, at least we'll have the satisfaction of trying."

"Meaning, at least you'll have had the chance."

"Yeah." Fred tossed his cigarette butt on the ground, scuffed it out with the sole of his boot, and looked Vance in the eye. "I'll tell ya, if you want to go along, it won't be much trouble for you. Just back us up, like I said. And you don't need to go to much bother to get ready. Just bring your bedroll and whatever you might need for yourself. We'll bring the grub and the stuff to cook with."

"What if we get out on the trail, and one day just keeps leadin' into the next?"

"This is goin' to be either-or," Fred answered. "Either we catch up with 'em, or we come back."

Vance lifted his gaze toward Tip, who had not gotten down from his horse. The young man had lost a brother and had come to ask a friend for help. He was mournful, bitter, and pleading all at the same time.

Vance took in the two brothers at a glance. They felt they were in the right, and they needed support — a little more weight, as Fred had put it. They were two against two right now, and if they could pick up a couple of men to side them, it might even discourage Rusk and the Mexican from shooting it out. And if those two turned out to be some kind of desperadoes, Fred and Tip could use the help.

"I'll tell you what," Vance said. "If you can get a fourth man, I'll go along. Otherwise, I don't like the odds so well."

Tip's face relaxed. "I think it'll work, Vance. We were plannin' to ask Shorty next, and if you go, I think he will."

"That's a good idea." Shorty had guts, and a good sense of humor to boot. And just as a matter of numbers, he and Vance could keep things in balance with the two brothers. "Why don't you go ask him, then, and if he says yes, I'll go."

Fred cleared his throat. "I'm pretty sure he'll go. And just to keep us from losin' any more time, I'd just as soon not have to come back by here a third time."

"How long will it take us to find Shorty?"

"Oh, not long at all," Fred answered. "We saw him in town, and he said he'd be there the rest of the day."

"Then you already asked him?"

"No, not really."

"But he knows what happened to Moon?"

"Oh, yeah. Everyone does. Everyone in town, anyway."

"And he knows what you've got in mind."

"Oh, kind of."

Vance turned down the corners of his mouth. Things were getting settled faster than he thought. "Well, let me talk to Josie. I'll be out in a few minutes."

Inside the house, Vance and Josie spoke in low tones to keep from waking the baby. Vance explained what the Dunham boys had come for, and Josie made no expression as she listened.

"So you're thinking of going, then."

"I think so. I'm not all the way sold on the idea, but Tip is a good friend and he could use the company. Especially if Shorty and I both go along."

"What if someone . . . gets hurt?"

"I think there's less chance of it if there's more of us."

She gave him a dead stare. "What if something happens to you?"

He shrugged. "Then I guess it does. But you can bet I'll do whatever I can to keep anything bad from happening to anyone."

She gave a slow nod. "Well, go ahead, if you think you have to."

"It's not that I think I have to, but that I think I ought to."

It was her turn to shrug. "I suppose it comes to the same thing. Do you want me to put up some food for you?"

"I don't think so. They say they'll take care of all that. I just need a bedroll and a few clean things. Just as if I'm going to a cow camp for a few days."

Within ten minutes he was ready to go. Josie stood in the kitchen with her hands clasped together in front of her. Vance saw her dark, shoulder-length hair and her blue eyes, and he remembered a time, a year ago and more, when he saw a pretty girl each time he looked at her, a time when she had all the magic of a woman in a dress. Now it was as if she was beyond his reach, as if a shield of glass had come between them. Her eyes that once reminded him of mountain lakes now seemed as impenetrable as the spots on willow-pattern china. He wondered how he could know less about a person than he once did, or thought he did.

After they had kissed good-bye and he was tying his bedroll onto the back of his saddle, he realized she had not questioned his decision or asked him not to go. As far as the two of them were concerned, she had seemed to have no more feeling than he did.

As he led the horse out into the bright sunlight where the Dunham brothers waited, he thought of the idea he had not mentioned to Josie — that a man should have a chance to get even when he had been done wrong. He didn't try to sort out the notion or decide on whose behalf any of them might be getting even. He just knew that it felt like the right justification for riding out together.

He glanced at the front door, half-hoping that Josie would appear, but she didn't. Instead of movement at the doorway, he saw the heap of rope by the step. He tied his horse at the hitching rail, then picked up the mess of rope and put it back in the stable. Even if things had gone cold with Josie for the time being, he wasn't going to leave his stuff around and have her pick up after him. Things had not changed in that way.

Back out in the warm afternoon, he checked his front cinch and swung into the saddle. Looking back at the door, he found it motionless again. Then he picked up his horse's pace and fell in with the Dunham brothers. He turned to his left and nodded at Tip, who gave a tight smile and a short nod. Further to his left he caught the glance of Fred, who wore a satisfied smile as he held up the first three fingers of his right hand.

Chapter Two

The breeze felt good in Vance's face as he loped toward Rock River with the Dunham brothers. Complications seemed to fall away behind him. The cattle would be all right for a few days without him, and there wasn't any job so pressing it couldn't wait. The same went for Josie. There was a time when leaving her alone caused the worry to bite deep into him, but that time had passed. As he knew from the times he had gone off to roundups and cow camps, she could take care of herself well enough; and even if she wasn't glad to see him gone this time, a few days on her own might do her some good. If it didn't lighten her glumness, at least she wouldn't have his presence weighing on her. And, of course, she had the baby to cheer her up.

Josie and the baby, cattle and fences and range boundaries and the faceless men who threw the wide loop — he could put it all behind him for a few days. Maybe up ahead this fellow Rusk and his Mexican *compadre* would cause some trouble, but

24

for the moment Vance felt a lightness of the spirit. The land flowed beneath his horse's hooves in a stream of grass, cactus, and sagebrush. Sometimes, like now, on a horse with a smooth lope, Vance felt as if he were floating. From the instant the horse broke into the lope until the moment when it would take the few jolting steps to slow down, Vance had the sensation of having been lifted from the ground.

Half a mile from town, the riders slowed their horses to a walk. As they rode into the main street at a slow, rocking gait, Vance took in the surroundings. The buildings sat calm and unchanged from the last time he had seen them. Moon Dunham wasn't the first man to die by gunfire in this town, and he wouldn't be the last. Stagecoaches had rumbled through here on the Overland Trail, and the railroad crews had built the U.P. line along this same stretch. Wherever rough men traveled and met, trouble was bound to flare up sooner or later. One man more or less wouldn't change the character of this town, even if a handful of people were in a stir about a recent killing.

Vance spoke up, raising his voice above the clip-clop of the horse hooves on hard-packed dirt. "Where are we supposed to be able to find Shorty?" he asked.

"In the Lariat," Fred answered. "He said he'd be sure not to budge from there."

"One thing about Shorty," said Vance. "He'll keep his word." He looked over at Tip, who smiled.

As Vance tied his horse to the hitch rack in front of the saloon and followed Fred and Tip inside, he had the sense of being in the public eye. Half a dozen men, including Shorty, were standing along the bar. They all turned to watch the Dunham brothers come in with their recruit. Shorty took half a step away from the bar and faced them, smiling, with his brown eyes wide open.

"Hello, boys. I see you made it back. And I see you managed to bring Vance along. Hello, Vance." He held out his hand.

Vance shook it. "Afternoon, Shorty. What do you know?"

"Water won't flow uphill, and the sun won't set in the east." Shorty stood in a relaxed pose, with his hat tipped back and his thumbs in his waistband. His red bandanna hung loose at his neck, his watch chain drooped across the front of his vest, and his six-shooter was slung on his right side as casually as a carpenter's hammer.

Shorty had the tough build of a cowpuncher, except that he was almost a head shorter than most men.

"That's a safe bet," said Vance.

"The best kind." Shorty smiled before he flicked his glance at the brothers. "Well what do you think, Fred? You still rarin' to go git 'em?"

"Vance says he'll go along if we can get a fourth. And it didn't seem to scare him too much that it might be you. So we're back, with the same idea. What do you think?"

Shorty dipped his chin down and up a couple of times. "I'm game," he said. Then he looked around at Vance and Tip. "How about you fellas? Do we have time for a drink?"

Vance shrugged, and Tip looked at Fred.

"Maybe a quick one. On me." Fred lifted his head toward the bartender and signaled with his hand to bring a round.

A jovial, round-faced man who looked like a drummer spoke up from behind Shorty's left shoulder. "You're not going to let these fellows drag you out of this nice saloon and into the cruel heat of the day, are you now, Shorty?"

"Looks like it." Shorty tossed the comment over his shoulder.

"I thought you said the girls got here at about sundown."

"They do, the last time I checked."

"And when was that?"

Shorty's eyes sparkled. "Yesterday."

A ripple of laughter went down the bar. The man in the suit spoke again.

"I think you're joshin' me. I was in here yesterday, and I didn't see you."

Shorty gave a sly smile. "Maybe you're right. It might have been the day before."

"Oh, I thought you said you were waitin' for the girls."

"Maybe I did, and maybe I was. But now I got somethin' else to do, so that stuff can wait. As far as I'm concerned, anyway. But don't you worry. You'll be able to get some mud on your turtle before you leave town, and you don't need me to introduce you."

The bartender set down a bottle and three glasses. Shorty slid his alongside, and Fred poured the drinks.

"Here's to it," said Shorty as the four glasses went up and touched. "And to them that can do it."

Fred tossed down his drink right away and told Tip to do the same. "Don't be in a hurry," he said to the other two. "We'll go get the grub and such, and we'll come back when we're ready to pull out. Won't be long."

As soon as the brothers were gone, Shorty stood back from the bar again. A smile played on his face, as if he were trying to decide whether to tell a joke he had in mind. "I like to think this is just a wild-goose chase," he said, "but it could turn out different. If it does, maybe between the two of us, you and me, we can keep Tip out of trouble."

"I hope so," said Vance. "But there's no guarantee we'll even catch those other two."

"No tellin'. But Fred's all het up to give it a try, and Tip's determined to go with him."

"That's for sure." Vance took a sip on his drink. "Say, Shorty, did I understand that you weren't in town last night?"

"That's right."

"So you didn't see any of what went on."

"No."

"Neither did Fred or Tip. Does anyone know what this fellow Rusk looks like?"

"They say he's got a beard."

"How about the Mexican?"

"I don't think he showed up until Moon and the other one, Rusk, had it out."

"Well, maybe they did jump him, then.

The first time I heard it, I thought they both called him out, but maybe just one of 'em did and the other one was waitin'."

"I don't know. But I wasn't surprised to hear that Moon had gotten into that kind of trouble."

"I guess I wasn't, either. It's just that he's dead."

"That he is. And if it was just for his sake, I wouldn't be going on this chase."

"Neither would I," said Vance. "But his brothers deserve something. Like Tip says, a fellow should have a chance to get even."

Shorty nodded. "I heard Fred say it, but I'd agree with either of 'em on it." He took out his watch. "Any way it works out, though, I hope they get back pretty soon, or we'll lose the whole day."

The brothers were gone for about half an hour, and then Fred appeared at the door of the saloon. "We're ready," he said.

Vance and Shorty finished their drinks and stepped outside onto the board sidewalk. Out in the street, Fred and Tip stood by their saddle horses, and Tip held the lead rope of a packhorse. It was loaded with a set of panniers and had a manty tied over the top.

"How much are you bringin'?" Shorty

asked as he and Vance stepped down from the sidewalk.

Fred spoke in his matter-of-fact tone. "It's not that much, so Tip and I put our bedrolls on top. He'll still keep up just fine."

Shorty looked at Tip. "Did you say good-bye to your girl?"

Tip nodded and looked down, then up again. "Yeah, I did."

"Well, that's good," said Shorty. "I suppose I can go get my horse, then, if I'm the one that's holdin' us up."

A few minutes later, all four riders were mounted and heading out on the main street. Three of them rode abreast — Fred on the left, Shorty in the middle, and Vance on the right — while Tip rode behind, leading the packhorse.

When they had ridden a couple of blocks, a young woman came out of a side street on the right and stepped up onto the sidewalk. Vance recognized the figure and the shape of her head. It was Ruth, Tip's girl. Her hair hung loose to her shoulders, rich and full, the color of dark straw. She waved to the three men in front, her brown eyes steady, and then as Vance rode past her, she turned to wave to Tip. Vance kept his eyes straight ahead, and he could see

31

that Shorty was doing the same.

When the moment had well passed, Vance looked across at Fred, who lifted his hat for ventilation and set it back on his head, then turned to face Shorty and Vance. He gave a nod and a wink and held up four fingers of his right hand. His horse picked up a fast walk and the others joined in. At the edge of town, Fred pulled his hat down tight before putting his horse into a lope. Then the whole group was moving together, out onto the plains west of Rock River.

The hooves drummed and the air brushed against Vance's face. He felt lifted again by the energy of the horses and by the surging movement of the animals in unison. He imagined it was the way soldiers felt when they set out in a troop, when the expedition was new and they were sure they were going after an enemy they could pummel. A man felt free and at large, cut loose from petty attachments and unbound by anything he would be passing through. If a skirmish lay ahead, he would worry about it when the time came.

Less than a mile from town, Tip called out and said they needed to tighten the packs, so the party came to a halt. Shorty and Tip dismounted to tend to the lashes, and Vance got down to hold their horses. Fred stayed in the saddle with both hands on the horn.

"Tighten 'em good," he said.

"Wouldn't do it any other way," said Shorty. "We'll git 'er tight as a whore's corset, eh, Tip?"

"Uh-huh."

Vance looked out across the country they had just left behind. Beyond the buildings of the town, he could see the roll of earth where Rock Creek ran to the northeast. Beyond that, a ridge with cedars on it angled north, and in back of it a long, bare ridge rose up and ran further north. A good thirty miles away, he knew, lay the Laramie Mountains, lost in the haze at this distance except for one broad peak that rose in faint purple. A little closer, in the opposite direction, would be the Medicine Bow Mountains. Vance could not see a bit of them at the moment, but he knew the mountains were there, capped in snow in the highest places. Not long ago — just a few years — he had been free to go to either of those mountain ranges, where he could listen to the wind in the pines and wash his face in a mountain stream. But for the time being, he had his work and his obligations here on the high plains — this wide, rolling country that was cold and windy in winter, hot and windy in summer. *Good in no season,* he recalled having heard one time.

Tip and Shorty had the job done in a few minutes, and the group got under way again, this time at a fast walk. As he rode along, Vance pictured the trail ahead as it ran northwest and then curved around to run west again into Medicine Bow, nearly twenty miles away. He wondered if they would make it all the way to Medicine Bow this evening.

A few miles out, he began seeing Elk Mountain to the south, clearer and closer than Laramie Peak earlier. Looming on the northeast edge of the Snowy Range in the Medicine Bow Mountains, it was the main landmark for fifty miles along this route, always on the left as the trail ran west. The country in between could vary from flatland to rolling hills to broken gashes, but a fellow could always get his bearings by riding to a high spot and finding Elk Mountain to the south.

At about eight or nine miles out of Rock River, the road curved around to the south end of a long, high ridge that came down from the north. Beyond the end of the ridge, the country turned rough and broken on the left and then gave way to stark mountains. The sun was slipping in the sky, and Vance began to wonder again if they would try to make it as far as Medicine Bow.

Dropping back and then riding around on Fred's left, he asked, "What's your idea on how far we're going to travel this evening?"

"As far as we can get."

"Well, what I mean is, do we expect to make it all the way into Medicine Bow, or should we be thinkin' about a camp out in the open?"

"Oh, I guess town would be best." Fred looked around at the outfit and made a frown. "But then we'd have the expense of puttin' up five horses and four men, before we even got twenty miles."

"All the same to me, but if you've got grub and all that —"

"That's what I was thinkin'."

"Maybe we should be on the lookout for a place to camp, then, before it gets too dark."

Fred looked out over the country ahead. "We should come to that little river before long. We can camp there."

The Medicine Bow River was a small stream, no bigger than a lot of creeks at this part of its journey, where it ran through the grassland. Only brush grew along its banks here, so a traveler couldn't see it from miles away as he could with a watercourse marked by trees. But it was a handy stream, cutting right across the trail and running enough water for a handful of men and horses.

The riders drifted downstream a hundred yards until they came to a spot where men had camped before. A broad, sandy slope ran down to the water's edge, and in the middle of the bare spot sat a fire pit lined with blackened rocks.

"We'll camp here," Fred announced.

Shorty lifted his eyebrows at Vance and said, "There's an idea."

The men all dismounted, and Vance held four horses as Tip and Shorty untied the packs.

"Wouldn't you know it," said Shorty. "No sooner do you start to pitch camp than clouds start to pilin' up."

Fred, who had been walking his horse around the edge of the campsite, seemed not to want to recognize the comment. In response he said, "We'll eat good tonight."

As Shorty coiled up the tie ropes, Tip laid the manty, or top canvas, on the ground and set a bedroll on each side to peg it down. Then he unloaded the panniers onto it, taking from each side a big slab of bacon wrapped in newspaper, which had the grease already showing through. Vance thought of his table back home, with the clean bowls of rice pudding. *Four days,* he thought. Four days of bacon and brackish coffee. He could feel it in his stomach already.

"We're gonna need some firewood," he said. "Shorty, how 'bout you and me goin' to find some?"

"Just what I was thinkin'," Shorty chirped.

Fred didn't seem to notice. "Go ahead," he said. "We'll get the camp set up."

Vance and Shorty untied their bedrolls, dropped them on the ground, and rode off upstream to look for wood. The clouds in the west were thickening, but there was still enough daylight for their chore. When they had ridden a ways out from camp, Vance spoke.

"We might wish we'd ridden on to Medicine Bow."

Shorty looked at the sky. "We might."

They had to ride upstream nearly a mile until they came to a place where the river wound through some low hills. There they found a few trees, mostly cedar, growing at liberal distances from one another. A few pieces of deadfall lay here and there. Shorty rode up to a branch that had its butt end clearing the ground. His rope sang, then slapped around the end of the branch, and he pulled his slack as if he were roping the heels of a steer.

Vance roped a branch for himself, tied off on his saddle horn, and headed back to the spot where Shorty waited. Then they put their horses into a fast walk toward camp.

"We might get wet tonight, Shorty. Maybe you'll wish you'd stayed in Rock River."

"Just might. It would've been a better way of gettin' wet."

Vance laughed. "That drummer, or whatever he was, seemed interested in the girls."

"Oh, yeah."

"He seemed to take you for a local expert."

"Well, you know, when these fellas ask questions, you like to have answers for 'em."

"Inquisitive sort, was he?"

"Pretty much so. He had questions about everything, like he wanted to hear the natives talk, so I tried not to disappoint him."

"That's good. I hope you gave him his money's worth."

"I might have. When he asked me if everyone called me Shorty, or just my friends, I told him everyone did except the girls, who never thought to call me that when I had my pants down. Told him it was always a good surprise for 'em."

Vance laughed. "So he looked at you the way some fellows would look at a good hunting guide."

"Somethin' like that, I guess. He figgered I could lead him to the good ones. But I didn't like to be humored, much less taken for a pimp, so I didn't mind leavin' him to fend for himself." Shorty lifted his head in a smile. " 'Course, there's always a good joke in just about everything, so I could've managed all right if I'd gotten stuck with him for the rest of the evening."

The wind was starting to pick up when they got back to camp, so the men made what windbreak they could with their bedrolls and got the fire going. Fred took out his jackknife and began to slice the bacon.

"Yeah, we'll eat good tonight," he said, scraping some blowsand off the cut end of the slab and then wiping his knife blade on his lower pants leg. "We'll eat good and sleep good, and then tomorrow we'll get after those sons of bitches."

No one else said anything, and the silence hung in the air.

"I know it doesn't mean as much to you two as it does to us," Fred went on, "but we all know one thing. These bastards went way over the line with what they did, and if anyone's gonna do right by Moon, it's got to be us."

Fred let out a long breath as he lifted in his crouch and started laying bacon slices in the two frying pans. As he handed the first skillet to Tip, he spoke again.

"The truth is, when you know you're in the right, and you know the other party's in the wrong, you've got the edge. You can whup the tar out of someone twice your size, and if it comes to shootin', your aim is better. Ain't I right, Shorty?"

"I 'magine. I don't know as I could whup the tar out of someone twice my size, though. Depends on who he is."

"But you know what I mean." Fred handed the second skillet to Tip. "If someone took your woman, or tried to, or did dirt to one of your kin, or — like in this case — out-and-out baited him and killed him, why, I know you'd be able to do plenty, knowin' you were in the right. And you too, Vance. You'd do something, and you'd be sure you were right, all the way."

Vance felt a pang of uneasiness. "I haven't had a brother die, because I haven't ever had one. But I had both my folks die, and even when you know it's comin' and you think you know what you'll do, you never really know how you'll feel or how you'll act until the thing happens. That's what I know."

"Well, I'm talkin' about things that shouldn't have happened to begin with."

Vance gave him a square look. "I know."

Shorty spoke up. "Well, we're here because of what happened to Moon — and to you two."

"That's right," said Fred. Then, swelling a little, he nodded his head and declared, "That's damn right."

Dark was setting in now, and the wind was not letting up. Vance and Shorty crouched next to Tip, the three of them with their backs to the wind, to try to provide some protection for the fire. Off to the left, where the camp gear was laid out on the canvas, Fred was rummaging through his duffel bag. At one point he paused, drew out his hand, and tilted the cupped palm toward the firelight. He had something in his hand.

41

Vance could not see it very well, but he could tell it was roundish and flat, bigger than a dried apple and darker. It went partly out of view as Fred rubbed his thumb on it a few times. Then Fred's hand went back into the bag and came out with a small sack of Bull Durham. Turning back to a crouch closer to the others, he began to build a cigarette.

Vance wondered about Fred's comments about whupping a man twice your size, getting even with someone for taking your woman, and evening the score for things that shouldn't have happened. He wondered if Fred was being deliberate, putting the problem in terms that Vance and Shorty could see themselves in — and if that was what he was doing, Vance wondered if Fred was still trying to persuade them to do something they had already agreed on or if Fred felt the need to keep justifying their course of action. Vance shook his head. Sometimes Fred just talked too much, regardless of what he was up to. What Vance needed to do was not let it get under his skin.

Fred spoke up as he finished rolling his cigarette. "Smells good already," he said as Tip poked at the bacon slices with his knife.

Maybe that was it, Vance thought. Fred was telling them what a good decision they had made. He was telling them that even if they had to sleep out in the weather, they would eat good tonight. And if he told them that, he could pretend that they believed it.

Supper consisted of bacon, cold biscuits, and hot coffee. The coffee had a bitter taste, and the bacon had grains of sand and flecks of campfire ash. As Vance ate his portion, he thought it didn't matter if they were eating good or not. Even if the gritty food was far from a soft, smooth serving of spotted puppy, it was better than no grub at all, and sitting in the wind out on the plains was better than Moon was doing: lying on his back in total darkness in the back room of the barber shop in Rock River.

Chapter Three

Vance could feel the grub in his stomach, but it sat all right. The bacon and coffee were not churning yet, not in the way he expected they would in two or three more days. He had a bit of an aftertaste but not enough to keep him from drinking a second cup of coffee. The scene around the campfire was quiet except for the wind, and each man seemed to have lapsed into his own thoughts. Shorty was cleaning his fingernails with a penknife, while Tip and Fred were staring at the fire.

Vance had drawn into himself and was still working over a couple of Fred's comments that he hadn't been able to put out of his mind. Fred had tossed out the remarks separately, but they ground together now like grit in the food. The first comment was the one about someone trying to take your woman, and the second was the one about things that shouldn't have happened to begin with. Maybe Fred didn't mean for his comments to run any deeper than references to his brothers and himself, but they had worked their way into Vance's thoughts and had made him sullen. The irritation started with the sense that Fred might be trying to work him, but even when he brushed off Fred as a nuisance, the comments themselves were still there.

People said time changed everything, but Vance wondered if time itself would do it. This problem with Josie should have gone away by now, but the residue stayed around. Even when he tried to leave it behind him, a few words from Fred — careless or artful, it didn't matter — brought it back and worked it up like bile.

There was a time when he thought he would like to kill Nate Cousins. Although he had no reason to feel that way anymore, he could remember the feeling all too well. He associated it with shiny gun metal, a six-gun wiped clean, the cylinder oiled and clicking between thumb and forefinger. Or long moments off by himself on the range, when he would pull the rifle from its scabbard, get a good rest on a rock or tree trunk, and line up the sights with a man-shaped target. Maybe it was just a fancy thought; maybe he would never have killed anyone. But even now, when all cause for worry was gone, he could remember thinking he had a right to do it if he wanted.

At less heightened moments, he reasoned with himself. He made himself admit that he had done something to help bring it about — he had taken her for granted, had left her at home for long stretches by herself, had been too tight-fisted to take her to Cheyenne or Denver when he might have. He also reasoned with himself that whatever she had done, she had done of her own free will. If she had an equal share of the blame, then the punishment, if any, should not all fall on the other man. Fair-minded thoughts at reasonable moments, they still did not keep him from acting out his resentment at some far-off place, where he would ear back the hammer of his rifle and practice settling the bead into the notch.

He couldn't have brought himself to try to punish Josie. He knew of men who did, and he had no idea of whether things had gone better or worse in those cases. In his own, things had gone dead from the moment he asked Josie whose watch this was and how it came to be here. From that time forward, she withdrew into her own world, as if she had a bubble of glass around her. Prior to that, he had felt as if there were no clear boundaries between them, as if they crossed over into one another's lives without restraint. Now she was all separate, beyond his reach, and even when he touched her, she stayed on her side and he stayed on his. He no longer lost himself in the sky-blue eyes, the mountain-dark hair, the hilly contours of her firm young body.

When it came to confronting Josie, he had felt powerless, but when it came to hating the other man, he found the strength to act. He went through her trunk, thinking he might find letters that he could vent his anger on. Finding none, he sneered to himself that maybe the fellow didn't know how to write. He found the time and the nerve to check on the man's holdings, to count his cattle, watch his cabin, and learn to recognize his horses. Vance had the notion that the more he knew about Nate Cousins, including the nature of the brands on his cattle, the more power he would have to do something about him. But in the end, that, too, remained only an idea.

Fred broke the silence by standing up, shaking his coffee grounds into the fire, and tapping the empty tin cup against his leg. "Pretty damn good, I'd say," he declared. He handed the cup to his brother and then sat down again on his bedroll. "We covered a fair piece of ground today," he went on as he began to roll a cigarette. "We get a good night's rest, and we'll be up and at 'em first thing in the morning."

A gust of wind lifted a cloud of ashes from the fire, and Tip turned one skillet upside-down over the other. "I might as well clean up the plates," he said, "and get a pot of water for coffee in the morning."

Vance looked at Shorty. "I guess we can go ahead and take care of the horses, then."

Shorty closed his penknife with a click and tucked it into the pocket of his trousers. " 'Magine so."

Earlier in the evening, they had watered the horses and staked them out to graze. Now they would water them for the night and set them back out on their pickets. If they had had any spare horses, they could have kept a night horse saddled and close in, but they decided to give each horse as much grazing and rest as possible, so they had all five to tend to.

Vance stood up and, feeling the wind rock his hat, pushed it tighter onto his head. Shorty got up and stomped his boots. Leaving Fred to sit on his bedroll and smoke a cigarette while Tip cleaned up the eating utensils, Vance and Shorty headed out into the darkness beyond the firelight.

When they got out of earshot of the camp, Vance walked close to Shorty. "What do you make out of Fred's comments?" he asked.

"Which ones?"

"The ones about these sons of bitches we're supposed to be trailin'. Does it seem like he's tryin' to make it personal to you and me?"

"Ah, I don't know. Not that I noticed."

"Well, he gets to soundin' awfully righteous."

"That he does. I wish he didn't try to make Moon into such a saint. Even if they got him unfair, that don't make him any better than he was."

"That's for sure."

The wind was blowing harder now than during supper, and the air smelled like rain. Vance could see the dim shapes of the horses as they moved around on their picket ropes.

"I'll untie 'em," said Shorty. "I think we'd better do 'em all at once."

"All right."

Shorty moved away and came back after about a minute. "They seem kinda jumpy," he said as he handed two ropes to Vance. "We'll do well to get 'em all set out again. Go ahead and take these two."

Vance looked closely at the two horses he held. One was his own and the other was Tip's. In the dark, with the wind blowing, two horses would be enough, and he didn't like to leave Shorty with such a handful. "Can you get the others?" he asked.

"You bet."

Vance had to lead the horses into the wind to get to the river's edge, and once he got them there, they kept shifting around as they tried to put their rumps to the wind as they drank.

Large raindrops started to fall as Shorty brought the other three horses down the bank. Vance could hear the drops slapping in the water and he could smell rain on dust, then rain on horsehair. The drops were hitting hard through his shirt and rattling on his hat.

Shorty's three horses were sashaying and snorting as he pulled them onto a level spot ten yards away. "Let's wait a minute and see how bad this gets," he called out.

Vance could see that the other three

horses had worked around so that they all had their hindquarters to the storm, and Shorty was hunched against the driving rain as well.

Then the drops began to sting, and Vance could see what looked like raindrops jumping up from the ground. Then it came down thicker, with a sound like running cattle. It was hail, sure enough. He moved his left hand up the lead ropes and held the horses' heads low, then stood in their lee as close as he could get. If the hailstones didn't get any bigger, he and Shorty might be able to wait it out.

Down came the hail, thick and noisy as it sliced into the water and thudded on the ground. A bolt of lightning showed Vance that the pea-sized stones were beginning to pile up. A few seconds later, another flash let him see Shorty, who had lost his hat but was still hanging on to the three milling horses.

Then the noise got louder and the stings got sharper. Vance could see hailstones as big as grouse eggs bouncing up from the ground. Much more of this and they would have to turn the horses loose and hunt for cover. Another bolt of lightning flashed, and he saw two of Shorty's horses charging up the bank. Then he heard Shorty holler out.

"Let 'em go! Ride one if you can!"

The storm was all a roar and a blur, with stones pelting Vance's face like the fists of a dozen bullies. When the lightning flashed again, he made sure he knew which horse was his, and he let the other one go. Then, grabbing a hank of mane with his left hand as he held the lead rope, and putting the flat of his right hand in the center of his horse's slick back, he scrambled up onto the stutter-stepping horse. Clamping on with his legs and leaning close to the horse's neck, he flicked his heels into the horse's flanks and hollered, "Go!"

The horse plunged up the bank and broke into a dead run, straightaway northeast. Let the horses go. That was the thing to do when a storm got violent. Some fellows said the horses knew which way to run. Maybe they did. Vance did know that a hailstorm would cover a path or a belt, pounding the hell out of trees and buildings in one area and not cutting a leaf in a luckier spot half a mile away. Shorty must have had the same idea: to ride out to the edge of the storm.

Lightning flashed above, and Vance could see open plains ahead of him, everything silvery white with falling and bouncing hail. He tightened his grip on the lead rope. If he fell off and lost the horse, he would have no cover at all. If he could hang on, the horse might be able to find its way out of the hail.

Vance held his head in low against the horse's neck, and he realized he still had his hat on. He wondered how Shorty was doing. If anyone could ride it out, it would be the tough little cowpuncher, but even the best horse and rider could take a spill.

The hailstones seemed to be stinging less now. Vance figured he had ridden about a mile, and he wondered if he was getting to the edge of the storm or out in front. It was all a guess to him, so he continued to let the horse choose its way. Onward it ran, with Vance hanging on like a bobcat.

More lightning flashed straight off to the right, followed by a sharp crash of thunder, and the horse cut to the left. Vance felt himself starting to slip on the right. He pushed against the horse's neck with his right hand and pulled on the mane with his left, which also held the lead rope. The horse moved beneath him, shifting to the right to help him stay seated. He bounced back up straight and then started to slip on the left. The horse broke its stride, and the gait got rougher, jostling Vance as he tried to hang on with his right arm and leg.

He hit the ground on his left side, still gripping the lead rope. Telling himself to hang on at all costs, he swung his right hand over and got a double grip. The forward momentum of the horse snapped him around and dug his right cheekbone into the damp grass and dirt. Then the horse went tumbling over with a grunt, spraying sand in Vance's face.

The two of them scrambled to their feet, and Vance stayed square in front of the horse while keeping a steady pull on the rope. The horse settled down. Vance could see it didn't want to fight. He just hoped it would let him get back on.

"Easy, boy. Good boy."

Lightning flashed again from back in the direction of camp, and the horse didn't flinch. Vance twitched his nose and smelled the air. Then he realized they had ridden out of the path of the hailstorm and were standing in the rain.

"Good boy," he said again, moving toward the horse and patting him on the flat, wet side of his neck. "Good boy."

After finding his hat where it had rolled off in the tumble, he took a few minutes to collect his thoughts. Somewhere out here on the plains, Shorty was either on foot or on horseback, and depending on how he had fared, either three or four more horses were scattered out beyond the reach of the storm. Most of the night still lay ahead, and there was no sense trying to find the horses until daylight. Vance figured camp to be somewhere between two and three miles to the southwest, so he faced that direction and watched the lightning. He imagined the campfire had gone out, but he thought he could find the place in the dark if he found the river and then followed it to camp. He would wait for the storm to pass, and then he could head west, hoping to come to the river somewhere north of camp. In the meanwhile, he decided, he needed to move around to keep up his body heat. His shirt was soaked, and he was starting to shiver. The best direction to go was away from the storm, so he turned north and began walking. Every once in a while he looked back over his shoulder to see how the night was progressing.

After about half an hour, stars began to show in the west. A little while after that, the moon, which was at half-full, came into view as the sky cleared overhead. Vance could see dark skies and occasional lightning farther east and to the south, which told him the storm had not played out. Finally warmer but still far from dry, he decided to keep walking as he turned west toward the river.

As he trudged along, he noticed the calmness around him. He and the horse made very little sound on the damp earth, and the air was fresh and cool, carrying the scent of wet sage. What a change, he thought, from the turbulence of an hour earlier. In daylight, the contrast after a storm was even more impressive, especially where there was more to damage. He recalled having seen trees, roofs, windows, and gardens all ravaged in the aftermath of a storm, while an innocent sky smiled overhead.

He found the river in the moonlight, running a little higher than before, he thought, but still flowing to his right. Leading the horse down to the water's edge, he let the animal drink. By now his feet were tired from walking in wet boots, so he positioned the horse next to a rise in the ground, stepped onto the high spot, and climbed onto the horse's back.

They followed the river for quite a ways. Vance thought he should have found the camp by now, but maybe he had ridden farther north than he realized, and maybe he had veered northwest on his way back to the river. The moonlight was good enough that he doubted he would miss the camp and all the gear, but even if he did, he would cut the main trail just a little farther south.

Then he came over a swell in the ground and saw the camp ahead on the left, not fifty yards away. Fred and Tip had a small blaze going, and they were crouched close to it. When Vance called out, they stood up to see him come in. They said he was the first they had seen of anything, man or horse, since the storm hit. Tip said it was after midnight and he expected to see Shorty come riding in before long.

Vance told his part of the story and then listened to the brothers. Tip said he managed to bundle up most of the camp gear and cover it with the panniers, but he got pretty well stung for the trouble.

"Fred was smarter. He took cover under a saddle right from the beginning."

Fred turned down the corners of his mouth. "It's the thing to do. You sure can't stop hail, so you'd best find cover."

Vance looked around the camp. "I suppose the bedrolls are all wet."

"Mostly the upper half," said Tip. "I didn't think of them until after I had the grub covered up, and by then I figured I'd better do like Fred."

"Oh, that's all right," Vance said. "A wet bedroll is nothing new, and I couldn't go to sleep right now if I wanted to. Shall we sit up a while longer and wait for Shorty?"

The others agreed. Tip said the fire was kind of slow because of the damp wood, but he would put on a pot of coffee. Vance took the horse out, put him on a picket, and came back to camp. Then it occurred to him to go down to the river and find Shorty's hat, which he did.

Shorty himself came into camp about twenty minutes later, just as the coffee pot was starting to send out steam. He was riding his own horse, bareback, and didn't look much the worse for the wear.

"You went off and left your hat," said Vance.

"I know. That's why I came back."

"See anything?"

"Probably about like you. At least we saved two horses. Maybe with them we can find the others when the sun comes up." He looked at Fred and Tip. "How did you boys make out?"

Shorty smiled as he listened to Tip's story. Then he said to Fred, "I reckon you didn't get to finish your cigarette."

"You're right. I didn't."

"Hell, Fred, for the little dab of hail we got, you could've covered your head with a fryin' pan and finished your smoke. But you dove under a saddle first thing, it sounds like."

Fred sniffed. "It was the normal thing to do. You never know how big the hailstones are going to get. And if your saddle's still on your horse, you get it off of him before he gets away from you. My respects to you two, but I wouldn't try to outrun a storm, especially at night."

"Well, both ways worked out," said Shorty. "We got somethin' to go hunt the others with in the mornin'."

"No harm done," Fred answered. "I'll bet you find all three."

Vance, having crawled out of a damp bedroll, sat at the edge of a smudgy fire as the bacon sputtered. He could see that Tip had used the last of the firewood to get up some breakfast. Shorty was inspecting his hat again by the first gray streaks of daylight, and Fred was standing at the edge of camp, looking east, as if the other three horses might have wandered back within view.

Tip spoke up from his crouch by the fire.

59

"I wonder if Rusk and the Mexican got hit by this same storm."

Fred turned and said, "It wouldn't hurt my feelin's if the hail got as big as melons and broke both their necks."

"No tellin'," said Shorty. "They might have woke up in a whorehouse in Rawlins." He smiled at Vance and then added, "Of course, anything that makes them lay around and kill time can help us catch 'em."

Fred was quick to answer. "You damn right we'll catch 'em, even with this delay."

Vance yawned, still trying to get himself going. If things went right, they should be back out on the trail by noon. "Say, Tip," he said. "Are you plannin' to spread the gear out to dry while me an' Shorty are gone lookin' for the horses?"

"Sure. I'll lay out all the bedrolls and everything. You fellas can get goin' as soon as you want."

The sun was just coming up when Vance and Shorty finished saddling their horses at the edge of camp. They each gulped a last half-cup of coffee at the fire, then swung aboard and rode out onto the plains.

Except for a few cut sprigs of sagebrush and a few pockmarks on bare dirt such as gopher mounds, a person couldn't see evidence of anything more than an overnight rain. The hail had all melted, and the ground was soft under the horses' hooves.

"Wherever they are, they should be settled down by now," Vance said.

"Oh, yeah," said Shorty. "It's just a matter of findin' 'em."

The riders split up, Vance going almost due north while Shorty rode northeast. An hour later, Vance saw a speck about a mile away to his right. As he rode towards it, he could see it was a horse, and then, riding closer, he saw it was Tip's. When he came within a hundred yards, the horse lifted its head and trotted away, holding its muzzle out to the left to let the rope trail along on the side. It played run-and-chase for another half-mile, until Vance circled around and rode straight at its front left shoulder. He had untied his coiled rope from the saddle, and now he swung out a loop. The other horse must have known the game was up, as he let himself be roped.

Vance got down from the saddle, gathered the lead rope, took his own rope from around the horse's head and coiled it again, and climbed back into the saddle.

Half an hour later, he met up with Shorty and the other two horses.

61

"Looks like you had the same kind of luck I did," he said.

"Easy as pie," Shorty answered. "Rode right up to 'em where they were grazing together."

Vance looked at the sky. "We made good time. We ought to be able to get Fred back onto the trail before noon." He yawned, then blinked his eyes and opened them wide. "It's goin' to be a long day."

"Yeah," said Shorty, "but we'll eat good tonight."

They both laughed, then kicked their horses into a lope. The others fell in alongside, and the whole bunch headed back toward camp.

Chapter Four

About halfway back to camp, Vance and
Shorty slowed the horses to a walk for a
while. Running and walking, the bunch
moved in unison. Vance could feel the col-
lective energy, and having it directed toward
the west again gave him the sense that things
were back on track. He still wondered if
Rusk and the Mexican would become anything more than hazy figures in a tissue of
story, but at least he and the others hadn't
gotten their purpose thwarted the first night
out.

Shorty was picking his teeth with a thin,
dry twig and had a pensive expression on
his face as the horses walked along.

"You've got a dangerous look on your
face, Shorty, like you were thinkin' of
something."

"Bad habit, much as I try not to. But I
was rememberin' somethin' I saw this
morning, before I come up on these
horses."

"Uh-huh. What was that?"

"A couple of fellows I don't like to see,

wherever they show up."

"Oh. Who are they?"

"Winslow and Ludington."

Vance felt a wave of caution and revulsion, as if he had just seen a snake. "Where'd you see 'em?"

"Just about straight over east."

"Any idea of what they were up to?"

"Nah, but they get paid to snoop, so it doesn't surprise me to see 'em over this far."

"Hmm." Winslow and Ludington went under the generous title of cattle detectives. Sometimes they worked alone and sometimes they worked together, doing odds and ends of work for a variety of cattlemen from Cheyenne to Rawlins and from the Colorado line to the North Platte Valley. For the most part they poked their noses around and intimidated smaller operators, but they were also credited with cutting short the careers of at least a half-dozen horse thieves and running-iron men. Vance had never had any trouble with them, but if they were in the neighborhood, he liked to know about it. "Which way were they headed?" he asked.

"No way when I saw 'em. They were settin' up on a high point with their backs to me, like two buzzards on a fence rail, watchin' the country to the south."

"Well, let's hope they've got somethin' to keep 'em busy."

"I imagine they do. I doubt they go anywhere except on business."

Fred and Tip stood at the edge of camp as Vance and Shorty rode in with the horses. Tip was nodding approval, and Fred wore a half-smile. "You made good time," he said.

"Just like bringin' in the milk cows," Shorty answered.

Fred turned to Tip. "Well, we can start gettin' packed."

Vance looked up and down the river's edge, where the blankets and canvas sheets from the bedrolls were draped on the highest bushes. "We'll get the horses watered," he said.

Within half an hour, the men had their camp rolled up and tied onto the horses. They took a last look around the campsite and headed back toward the main road.

As they reached the trail, they met a lone rider coming from the east. He raised his hand, then put his horse into a jog to catch up with the waiting party.

"I wonder what he wants," Fred muttered.

Vance watched the man as he rode closer. From the way he bounced, he didn't look like a cowpuncher. He wore the nondescript clothes of someone who was used to the country and to traveling in the outdoors, but he didn't have the boots and spurs of a horseman or the muscle of a laborer. He was an average-sized, slender fellow with reddish brown hair and a flat-brimmed hat. He used both hands to rein his horse, and a pair of light leather gloves covered whatever an observer might be able to tell from a man's hands.

"Howdy," he said as he brought his horse to a stop.

"Same to you," said Shorty, who was closest.

"Is this the road to Medicine Bow?"

"One of 'em," Shorty answered.

"Oh? What are the others?"

"There's one comes up from the south, one comes down from the north, and another comes in from the west. It's a regular hub of a place."

The stranger, who had narrow brown eyes and a protruding, pointed nose and mouth, tensed his features and then smiled with his mouth closed. "Oh. I see."

Fred spoke up. "Goin' that way, I suppose?"

66

The man turned toward Fred. "Yes, I am. Mind if I ride along?"

"Not at all, if you can keep up."

The stranger smiled and showed a set of teeth that, in combination with his recessed chin, gave Vance the impression of a weasel. "Thanks. When I'm in country I don't know, I like to travel with company when I can." The man gave Fred a nod of appreciation.

"Good enough. I'm Fred Dunham. This is my brother Tip. These here are Vance and Shorty."

The traveler nodded to each in turn, but he seemed to have found his preference in Fred. "Name's Prophet," he said. "Emerson Prophet."

Fred, who had drawn back his shoulders, tipped his head and said, "Is that Profit, as in profit and loss, or is it Prophet, as in the Mormons an' them?"

"More like the Christian prophets, as far as words go. But among friends, I'd just as soon go by Em." Then, catching Fred's uncertain look, he added, "For Emerson."

"Oh, of course." Fred glanced around at the group. "Well, we'd better get movin'. Fall in where you want, Em."

Tip waited with the packhorse as the others moved ahead. Fred rode to the front, and Em stayed off to the side until Vance and Shorty fell in behind Fred. Then Em took his place in front, next to Fred. As he did so, Vance observed that the man was wearing a six-gun and had a regular warbag tied across the back of his saddle.

As they rode along, Vance noticed Shorty pressing his fingertips against various spots on his face and neck. As Vance had been doing the same thing earlier, he figured Shorty was feeling the places where he had been stung by hailstones.

"That hail has got some bite to it, hasn't it?"

"It sure has," Shorty answered. "I think I'd rather get bit by skeeters." He smiled at Vance. "Did you notice, though, that when it comes down like that, the skeeters go away?"

"Didn't think to notice."

"One of the small benefits. That and snakes. They say wild animals know when a storm's comin', and they hunt their holes."

"I guess they do. You see deer feedin' out in the middle of the day before a storm, too."

"Yep. You'll hear tall tales about the fella who takes shelter in a cave and has to share it with a snake, a bobcat, and a coyote, and they're all on good behavior because they're all hidin' from the same thing."

"Uh-huh." Vance wondered if Shorty was going somewhere with his line of talk, so he didn't add anything this time.

"Same thing when you crawl under a saddle, only there's not as much room there. I always look first, to make sure there's no snakes."

Vance let the silence ride for a few seconds, and then Fred spoke in Em's direction. "Shorty's talkin' about a hailstorm we had last night. Did you get any of it?"

"Not at all," said Em. "I spent the night in Rock River. When I got out on the road this morning, I saw where it had rained last night."

"You must have got an early start," said Shorty.

"I did."

"See any Indians?"

Vance thought Shorty must be playing on Em's remark that he didn't like to travel alone. There were no Indians to speak of for a hundred miles.

"No, I didn't. You're the first travelers I've met today."

"Well, it was a hell of a storm," said

Shorty. "Scattered our horses and put out Fred's cigarette."

Em looked at Fred, who said, "Shorty got a few knots on his head, and I think he wishes he'd stayed in the Lariat."

"That's a saloon in Rock River," Shorty tossed out.

"I believe I saw it."

The party rode on for about an hour, up over a rise and ahead on the plains, with Elk Mountain in clear view to the south. On the outskirts of Medicine Bow, they stopped at a roadhouse.

Fred went inside by himself, leaving his horse with Vance and Shorty. They watered their horses and Fred's at the trough, then drew aside to let Tip and Em water the other three. When that chore was finished, Em said he was going to go inside, too, so he left his reins with Tip and went in.

"I don't mind the fellow," said Tip, "but I wonder how long we'll be stuck with him."

"Maybe a while," Vance offered. "He and Fred seem to get along."

Tip looked at the door of the roadhouse. "Well," he said, "sooner or later he'll find out what kind of business we're on, and I wouldn't expect him to have much stomach for it. But then again, Fred told him he could ride with us."

"That's Fred," Shorty said.

Tip gave him a quick look. "What do you mean?"

"Oh, not much. But you ought to know as well as anyone that Fred likes to get other people to do what he's doin'. How many times have you been goin' to do somethin', and then Fred gets you to do somethin' else?"

After a few seconds, Tip said, "Quite a few, I guess."

"Well, Fred's your brother, and I don't want to say anything unkind about him, but he's got his little ways of tyin' up other people's lives and makin' his problems theirs."

Vance thought he could hear a mild warning that Shorty was making for Tip's benefit but that wasn't making its effect.

"Do you mean you wish you hadn't come along, then?" Tip asked.

"No, that's not it. But as for your question about how long this Prophet might tag along with us, I wouldn't be surprised if Fred just takes him in. It's Fred's way, to get others drawn in to what he wants to do."

"Well, I just don't know how much good

it does to have him taggin' along."

"Neither do I. He seems like he ought to be pimpin' some place, but I'm not the one to shake him loose."

"Neither am I," said Vance. "But like Tip says, maybe when he gets the idea that we're followin' a couple of killers, he won't be so fond of our company."

After a good while — long enough to have a couple of drinks, by Vance's calculations — Fred and Em emerged from the roadhouse, squinting against the bright light of day. Fred had a bottle wrapped in newspaper, and without comment he tucked it into his saddlebag. Then he looked at the group and gave his report.

"They say they ain't seen no white man with a Mexican. There's been plenty of men through here, includin' some with beards, but none with a Mexican. Shorty, you still remember what their tracks look like, don't you?"

"Yeah, but it don't do much good when there's been a storm come through in the meanwhile."

Fred shook his head. "They had to have come at least this far. They could've gone any of three ways once they got here, but my bet is they kept goin' west. Wouldn't you think so?"

Tip spoke up. "Makes as much sense as any other."

"I'd say it's an even bet, any of the three ways," said Shorty. "If they think someone's followin' 'em, they might expect the posse — or us, in this case — to count on their goin' straight west, in which case cuttin' to the north or south would be a smart move."

"We could ask in another place," Vance offered. "The folks in the hotel probably have a good view of everyone who goes by, unless it's at night."

"It's worth askin'," said Tip. "Won't take but a minute, and it's right up ahead."

"All right." Fred had a relenting tone in his voice. "Let's go, then."

The group rode ahead for half a mile and stopped at the hotel, where Fred went in to make his inquiries.

"I'll think I'll go across to the train station," said Shorty. "Won't do any harm to ask there as well."

Em said he would go into the hotel to keep Fred from staying too long. Vance looked at Tip, and neither of them said anything until Em was inside the hotel.

"What do you think he's up to?" Tip asked.

"I don't know. He either likes to eavesdrop or likes to drink with Fred."

Shorty came riding back across the road at the same time that Fred and Em came out of the hotel.

"Well?" Tip asked.

"Still nothin'," Fred announced. "Same as before. No one's seen a white man with a Mexican. But I know the sons of bitches had to come through here. You know, sometimes I think people lie because they don't want to get in the middle of things. They know someone's on the run, and they don't want to be the one to tell on 'em, out of fear that they'll come back and get 'em. That's what I think."

"Did you tell these folks that the white man and the Mexican were on the run?" asked Vance.

"Well, no, not really. But if someone's askin', people can figure out why. Maybe they're afraid of the Mexican."

"So what do you want to do?" asked Tip. "Follow your hunch and keep going west?"

Vance looked at Shorty, who had his eyebrows raised. "Let's see if Shorty found out anything."

Tip turned to Shorty. "Well, what about it?"

"No one's seen a Mexican, so that part's the same. But a man with a beard did come by, by himself."

"When was that?" Fred broke in.

"Yesterday morning. He came in by himself, from the east, and he asked for directions. Then he rode back the way he came."

"By God," said Fred, "he's keeping the Mexican stashed. And with good reason. He'd stick out like a nigger's toe."

Vance spoke to Shorty again. "What kind of directions did he ask for?"

"He was interested in the road west and the road south, and when he got the layout of how the two roads ran, he asked for more details about the one to Elk Mountain."

"The road south?" Fred insisted. "Not Elk Mountain Station, but the mountain?"

"The mountain," said Shorty. "And Rattlesnake Pass beyond that, and Warm Springs."

Fred's face lit up. "Well, by God, that's the best lead we've got so far. What do you think, Shorty? Did you get the idea that that's where he was headed?"

"That's where he was askin' about. Chances are, he went that way — after skirtin' this town, of course."

"Him and the Mexican," Fred added. "I'll tell you what. We can follow this road south, and sooner or later we'll go past wherever that storm came through. And then we might be able to pick up their trail again. What do you think, Shorty?"

"I think it's a good bet."

"All right." Fred seemed to be brimming with confidence again. "We might as well set out. Does anyone know this road?"

No one spoke at first, and then Shorty said, "I haven't been over it, but I did get directions. We go out of town about a mile or so, and the road forks. We veer off to the right and follow it through big rolling country. The Medicine Bow River is two or three ridges to the east, and the trail crosses the river damn near a day's ride south of here. After that, it follows on the left side of the river until the country opens up, and then you're lookin' square at Elk Mountain."

"That sounds clear enough," said Fred. "Let's water the horses and get goin', then."

Tip spoke. "We watered 'em about twenty minutes ago."

"Then I guess we're ready." Fred turned to Em. "Well, I guess you're on your own now."

"I don't mind goin' this way with you fellas," said Em. "If you don't mind the company."

"Well, where the hell are you goin', anyway? I just assumed you were going west."

"I am. I want to get to Warm Springs, and from what Shorty says, you're going in that direction."

"And you're not worried about any trouble that might come up along the way?"

Em smiled and showed his close-set teeth, then glanced around at the company. "Not with these odds. That Mexican will have to be a hell of a good shot to get to me."

Fred paused and then said, "Well, come along, then. It's not your fight, so you don't have to get into it if you don't want."

The tagalong smiled again. "That was how I saw it. I can keep to myself if it comes to it. But I can assure you of one thing." He patted the handle of his six-gun. "No Mexican is going to shoot me on this trip."

Vance thought the man had some kind of nerve, but he wasn't sure what kind if he didn't like to travel alone. Maybe his courage was a bluff.

Fred looked around at the rest of the group. "Unless someone's got a better idea, then, I guess we head south."

The company moved out as before, with Fred and Em in front, Vance and Shorty in the middle, and Tip with the packhorse in the rear. They rode south from Medicine Bow, went right when the road forked, and soon enough found themselves in the country Shorty had mentioned. It was big, rolling country with broad dips and high rises. Except for the sharper ridges and bluffs to the east where a few trees dotted the crests, it was treeless country, with shorter grass than Vance had been seeing. Down in the low spots, when Elk Mountain went out of view, he had the sense of being lost in the big folds of the country, with even less certainty than before whether the other party was ahead of them on this trail, and if so, how far. Out on the plains between Rock River and Medicine Bow, at least a man could tell when someone was not on the trail ahead; but in these large wastes, a man never knew when he was going to top a rise and be looking down the gun barrels of Rusk and the phantom Mexican.

Every rise proved to be the same, though, giving way to one more empty stretch of land. Nothing moved in the heat of midday, and none of the men in the little party spoke. Then, about an hour and a half out of Medicine Bow, Shorty pulled out to the left, spurred his horse ahead of the others, and trotted along, looking at the ground. When he stopped his horse and the others came up and spread out, he looked at Fred and spoke.

"We're finally seein' tracks from before the rain. I believe we've come south of where the storm passed through."

"I think you're right," Fred declared. "There's not been many riders on this road. All along it's looked like we're the first ones since the rain, and now we've got some tracks that look a day or two old. See anything familiar?"

Shorty moved his head up and down. "I believe I do. These two sets on top look like the ones we picked up and followed to begin with."

A look of satisfaction spread across the dull gloss of Fred's face. "By God!" he said. "All we've got to do is catch 'em."

"That's right," said Shorty. "There's not a lot of water on this stretch, and I imagine they're bein' careful. But whether they are or not, we need to be."

"You damn right," Fred answered. He had a gleam in his eyes as he looked at the trail ahead. "You damn right. We won't make any mistakes."

At mid-afternoon they found water in a tiny creek that ran eastward. As they let the horses drink, Vance gazed at the high, bare ridges to the east. He thought it must be rough country out there, or the trail would follow closer to the river.

"Tell me, Shorty," he said, motioning his head toward the rugged slopes. "That little river we camped on, it's the same one that flows by Elk Mountain, and it goes out through those mountains, or hills, off over there. Is that right?"

"That's what I understood."

"It must flow between a couple of those ridges, then."

"I'd imagine."

"Must be rough gettin' in and out, or too narrow in some stretches, or the road would run closer to it."

"Makes sense. They said it was real rough in some places back there. I've never been down this way to know for myself."

"Me neither. I've been down and around the other way, by Quealy Dome, and out to the Snowies that way, and I've gone around the other way, followin' the railroad, but this is strange country to me."

Shorty gazed away at the barren land. "Me, too."

In the late afternoon, the road and the

high ridges to the east seemed to be coming together. Twice the party detoured to see if the river was near, but each time they found nothing but a dry wash.

"I don't think we'll hit the river today," Shorty said as they surveyed the bare rocks and dry gully at the second detour.

Fred looked at the sun in the west. "Yeah, we're just losin' time," he said.

Late afternoon was slipping into early evening when they found another creek bed near the road, this time with a narrow trickle of water in its bottom. Above it to the east ran a high brown ridge with cedars and scrub pines scattered along its crest. Beyond that ridge, thought Vance, or perhaps beyond two more just like it, ran the river. For the time being, this little dab of water would have to do.

The party made camp on the west side of the creek, in the long shadows of a ridge of pocked sandstone. It was a low formation, but it would give protection against any weather that might blow up from that side. From the looks of the sagebrush flats nearby and the hills beyond, this part of the country had not seen much rain since the spring.

As the men stripped the horses and laid the gear on the ground, Vance and Shorty collected the horses and made ready to take them to water.

"I'll take my own," Em announced.

"Ah, let them do it," Fred told him. "They're takin' the others. You can go hunt up some firewood. There's plenty of dead sage around here."

Em scowled and handed his lead rope to Vance, who with three horses followed Shorty and the other three down to the creek. When they came back up to camp fifteen minutes later, after staking out the horses, they found Fred seated on his bedroll with the whiskey bottle between his feet. Tip had rearranged the rocks of a fire pit, which the last travelers had apparently kicked in to snuff their fire, and Em was coming in with an armload of dry sage wood. Without much ceremony, he dropped it by the fire pit.

Fred's voice came out in the tone of a casual command. "Better get some more. That stuff burns pretty quick."

Em looked at the bottle and then at Vance and Shorty. "I wouldn't mind sittin' down for a few minutes."

"Go ahead," said Shorty. "Rest yer bones. Me 'n' Vance can go git some."

Em didn't answer but went to sit on the bedroll nearest Fred. Vance saw that it was

Tip's bedroll, and he wondered how much bedding the tagalong had in his warbag.

When Vance and Shorty came back with the rest of the night's fuel, Tip had a fire going. Fred and Em were seated at right angles to one another, and the bottle stood on the ground between them. Fred was holding forth.

"The thing that just cuts me to the quick, in addition to everything else, is how this son of a bitch Rusk doesn't respect another man's marriage. What kind of a man is that? A pretty low one, I'd say. And who knows about the son of a bitch that's sneakin' around with him? Probably afraid to show his face 'cause it's on 'wanted' posters."

Em nodded and reached for the bottle.

"But I'll tell you, I don't give a damn what kind of a cutthroat he thinks he is. When you're in the right, you've got the edge. They're on the run, and they know they're in the wrong, whether they want to admit it or not. And we've got 'em four to two." Fred swelled up and reached out for the bottle.

Em handed it to him. "Or five."

"Maybe they'll see it as five. But you didn't sound very game to fight, so I put it at four to two." The cork squeaked out of

83

the bottle, and Fred tipped himself a drink.

"Don't think I haven't any guts."

"I didn't say that. I was just goin' on what you said."

Em didn't answer, and Fred leaned back to haul his duffel bag around. Vance had noticed that Fred didn't smoke out on the open range, so he expected Fred to be rummaging for his Bull Durham. Instead, Fred brought out the dark, round object from the evening before, and as he had done on that occasion, he held it on the flat of his fingers and rubbed it with his thumb. The object came barely into view, as Fred kept his hand in the opening of the bag. Then he put the little thing away and brought out the cigarette makings.

His face had a dull, relaxed look on it as he paid attention to his work of rolling a smoke. After licking the seam and tapping it, he sat up straight and swelled his chest as he lit the cigarette. As he blew away the smoke, he said, "I wouldn't be surprised if we catch 'em tomorrow."

Em leaned forward to reach for the bottle.

"Go easy on that. It's gotta last."

"Oh, there's more where it came from. And from what you say, you'll be done with this business tomorrow."

A surly look crept onto Fred's face. "Maybe so and maybe no. It just seems to me that you're more help at emptyin' the bottle than anything else."

"Like what?"

"Well, like gatherin' firewood, to begin with."

"I did my share."

"You did some."

"What else, then?"

"Well, fightin'."

"You yourself said it wasn't my fight."

"You probably like it that way."

"What do you mean by that?"

"You want to ride along for protection, and anything you can mooch, but when it comes to a fight, it's not yours."

"Don't be so sure."

Fred took a slow drag and let the smoke drift out of his mouth. "I don't think you've got it in you," he said as he left the cigarette in his mouth.

"You don't know much."

Fred surprised Vance with the quickness of his move as he lurched forward, snatched Em by the front of his shirt, and pulled him close, rising to his feet. With the cigarette dancing in his mouth, he said, "Don't you be so sure about what I know or don't know, you understand? A little bit of your sass goes a long way. I don't think you even know how much fight you've got in you, and I don't think you want to find out now. Am I right?"

Em's face had dropped into an expression of dislike, and his eyes were flickering with worry. "You're right about that," he said. "We can save any fighting for Rusk and the Mexican."

The mention of their projected enemy seemed to placate Fred. He relaxed his grip on Em and let him settle back onto his seat. "Good enough," he said. Then he turned and walked away from the camp. About thirty yards out, he stopped with his back to the others in a recognizable pose.

Vance and Shorty, who had been standing on the other side of the fire, looked at each other without speaking. Then Shorty twisted his mouth and turned toward the fire.

"Say, Tip," he said. "What's that chingus that Fred carries around in his bag? Looks like a dried fig or something."

Tip looked up from poking at the fire. "It's his lucky charm."

"Oh." Shorty pushed out his lower lip and said nothing more.

Em spoke up from his side of the fire.

"Who knows but what he might need it." Then, as if he thought he should clarify, he added, "He's pretty sure we'll catch up with Rusk and the Mexican tomorrow."

Chapter Five

Vance sat on his bedroll and watched as Fred opened five cans of tomatoes with his jack-knife. In spite of his tendency to be over-bearing, Fred followed a code of fairness in his own camp. Whether it was a chuck wagon, a line shack, or a little trail camp such as this one, one man didn't begrudge another a place to light and a share of the grub. Vance had counted the cans of tomatoes the night before, and he saw that Fred had bought a dozen — one for each man for each full day they expected to be on the trail, he imagined. Canned food was handy at midday, when a fellow didn't want to take the time and trouble to build a fire. But Fred had been in a push ever since they left Medicine Bow, and he didn't make a noon stop or break into the packs. Instead, he passed around a few pieces of jerky, which he said he had bought in the hotel. He also assured everyone that they would eat good tonight, and he was making good on the promise now. Vance wondered if Fred had been reluctant to bring out the to-matoes at midday because it would upset the even number of cans, or if it was just a matter of being in a hurry. Whatever the case, Fred wasn't skimping now, even if the count would be off.

Fred wiped his hands on his pants, then did the same with his knife, and went on to slice the bacon. Again, he cut five full portions. When he was done, not much remained of the first side of bacon. Vance could see that at this rate, with an extra mouth to feed, the food supply wasn't going to last long.

He waited until Fred had wiped off his knife blade a second time, and then he spoke. "I'll tell you, Fred. When Shorty and I were gatherin' wood, we saw some antelope over on the flat across the creek. I was just thinkin' we could use a little more grub. I could sneak over there and see if I could pop one off."

Fred wrinkled his nose. "They're kind of stinky sons of bitches, and the meat don't keep well. Sounds like a lot of trouble."

"Oh, it wouldn't be that much. I think there's time before nightfall to give it a try."

"Sounds like a lot of bother."

"Well, it won't be to you. Shorty and I'll do all the cleanin'. Right, Shorty?"

"Fine with me."

Fred demurred. "I don't know if we want to be touchin' off shots. We don't know how close we are to those other two." He motioned with his head in the general direction of the trail they had been following.

"They were a full day ahead of us in Medicine Bow," Shorty said. "I doubt that we've closed the gap that much so far."

"Ah, hell. Do you what you want. You're like a couple of kids."

Vance looked at the two skillets, where the bacon was already curling and sizzling. "What do you think of saving some of the grease in one of those cans, Tip?"

"Be a lot of trouble to pack."

"No, I mean just for the morning. After that, we can melt a little bacon each time and fry the meat in that. If we get some."

Fred cut in. "Lot of bother for some stinkin' goat meat, I'd say."

Vance was tempted to comment on what was a lot of bother and what wasn't, but he checked himself and said, "It's grub."

"You've got to kill one first," Fred retorted.

"We'll give it a try." Vance looked at Tip. "Will you save some grease, then, just in case?"

"Sure. It's not that much trouble if I

90

don't have to pack it."

Vance and Shorty made quick work of their supper, then took off their spurs and pulled out their rifles. With light steps they made their way down into the creek bottom, which was cut like a canal about eight feet deep and thirty feet across. The stream itself was about a foot wide and a few inches deep, running down the middle. Their plan was to use the cover of the creek bottom to get closer to the antelope and then to make the best approach they could. Vance took the lead, carrying his rifle at his side with the barrel pointed forward.

He took the softest steps he could, avoiding rocks and gravel, crossing and recrossing the creek wherever the path looked quieter. With his eyes fixed most of the time on the ground ahead of him, he was startled when he walked around a curve in the stream bed and saw a gray-brown shape bound away from him. Without putting a thought or a name to it, he recognized it as a deer, and as his rifle came up, he saw the black tip of the tail, the sleek body, the big ears, and the spike antlers in velvet. The young buck ran thirty yards, turned right on a slope that went up the creek bank, and paused to look back.

Vance was following with the rifle sights, trying to pick up the right shot, and when the deer stopped, he brought the sights back to the lower part of the rib cage behind the deer's front shoulder. When everything came into place, he pulled the trigger.

As the shot died away, the deer slumped. Its legs went out from under it as it flopped on the slope and then rolled back into the creek bottom. Vance could see the dark chest and pale underside as the animal lay with its legs stretched out. Blood glistened from the hole in the ribs, and Vance knew he had made a good shot.

He turned to Shorty. "How about that? Go huntin' for one thing, and find another. I wasn't going to pass it up."

"Hell, no," said Shorty. "Easier to kill, and better meat."

They walked forward, and when they got to the fallen deer it was done kicking.

"We can dress it right here," said Vance. "Then if you want, you can go back and get a horse to pack him in on." He leaned over to pull the deer onto a level spot.

As Shorty held up a front and a back leg, Vance went to work with his pocket knife, opening the cavity and letting the loops of intestine roll out.

"Fred shouldn't have anything to complain about with this," he said.

"Oh, leave it to Fred. If he wants to, he'll find something to gripe about."

"Yeah, I think he's found every angle he could for criticizing Rusk. Not that I blame him for having a grudge, but he doesn't let it be."

"Isn't that the truth? I was sort of tickled when he was givin' Em the sermon about one man not respectin' another man's marriage."

"Uh-huh. Say, I think I need to rinse my hands and roll up my sleeves."

"Go ahead. I'll just hang onto this fella."

When Vance got his hands back inside the deer, Shorty resumed his topic.

"Yeah, I thought it was amusin', Fred carryin' on with someone who didn't know him."

"Uh-huh."

"I don't think he could've told me the same thing with a straight face. Maybe he could have, but I've known of times when Fred wasn't so respectful of marriage himself. As far as his intentions went, anyway, even if he didn't get to carry through."

"Oh, there's plenty of men like that."

"I'd say. A stiff prick has no conscience. If they get a chance, they don't think about

93

anything. It's like these boys when their necks swell up."

Vance looked at the spike antlers. "Yeah, this fellow was just a young one, but he'd have been the same." Then, thinking back to the scene at camp, he said, "I have to admit, there was a bit of humor in seein' Em just sittin' there, noddin', for the sake of chummin' up with Fred and the bottle, and even that could only go so far. The smart aleck came out eventually."

"I don't think he knew what to do when Fred grabbed him. His pride came up, and there he was, with not enough to back it up."

"It's the type of thing you try not to let happen. That is, you try not to let it get that far."

"Yeah, but if it does, I don't think I'd let someone push me around that way." Then, as if he thought he'd said enough on that subject, Shorty spoke in a louder voice. "Let me drag this fella uphill a little so you can let the blood run out of him."

"I don't know if anyone wants the heart and liver, but I'll cut 'em out and save 'em."

"No harm. And it looks like everything's comin' out clean."

Dusk was gathering when Shorty left to

go get a horse. He and Vance agreed that he should bring just one, as they were close enough to camp that it would take more time to saddle the other horses than they would save by riding back. Vance said he would wait with the deer, to keep critters off of it, so he sat down to rest as Shorty trudged away.

He looked again at the deer he had shot, and his thoughts went from one thing to another. He wondered about some of Shorty's offhand comments. The tough little cowpuncher didn't have much guile, but he was capable of subtlety. Vance thought for a moment that Shorty might have been telling him something about Fred's attempts with married women. No, he thought, Josie did not care for Fred at all, and she wouldn't have let him get close enough to make a pass. On the other hand, Vance knew that when a man had an inkling that a woman was up to something on the side, he sometimes got the idea that he could do a stroke of business there himself. Fred's comments suggested he might have had such an inkling, and Shorty's remarks suggested that Fred might have tried to act on it. Vance shook his head and took refuge in what he thought he could trust in Josie. Even if she had had something to do with Nate Cousins, she would have found Fred repugnant in any circumstance, so it didn't matter whether he tried something or not.

As for sniffing after other women and not getting anywhere, Vance had to admit he had done some of that himself. An older woman in Laramie — older by his standards, but still firm enough to put some fire in him — listened to enough of his story to give him some good advice. She said that if he had troubles with his wife, there was a good chance he had contributed to them, and he wasn't going to make things any better by trying to get even. He had tried it before and had even succeeded, so he knew what Shorty meant about a stiff prick having no conscience, but his conversation with the woman in Laramie left him with wilted intentions. As he thought of her now, she still shaped up as desirable, but he appreciated her having kept the distance between them. And he appreciated her advice. Getting even on that level wasn't going to make things better.

The sound of hoofbeats up on the flat brought him back to the moment, so he stood up and watched as Shorty came into view, putting the spurs to his horse and pushing him down the creek bank.

"You made good time."

"Tried not to waste any. It's gittin' dark."

"Mosquito time."

"That's right. Don't slap 'em, or the Injuns'll hear you."

Vance laughed. "How about the rifle shot? Were the others surprised we got something so soon?"

"They said it sounded kind of muffled, and they thought maybe someone fell on his gun."

"It's good that it didn't carry too far. If Rusk and the Mexican are just over the next hill or two, they wouldn't have heard much."

They got the deer tied onto the saddle, Shorty holding the horse's head as Vance hoisted the carcass and tied it so it wouldn't flop. Then they led the horse up out of the creek bottom and onto the sagebrush flat. Evening was closing in now. Back in camp, they unloaded the deer near enough to the fire that Vance could skin it by firelight. Fred didn't pay much attention, but Tip and Em came over to look at the animal.

"Looks fine," said Tip. "Should be good eatin'." He went back to the fire, while Em stayed to watch.

Vance cut off the forelegs and skinned the two hindquarters down to the pelvis. Shorty came back from putting the horse away, and he took over the job of holding the deer's legs up and moving the carcass one way or another as Vance needed it.

All this time, Em stood by and watched. "This isn't the first deer you've killed. I can see that."

"No, it isn't."

"How many have you killed?"

"Oh, I wouldn't know. I haven't kept track. Between them and antelope, I guess I've killed a few each year for the last ten years or so."

"You don't keep a little tally book, then."

"No, I don't. But even if I did, I probably wouldn't write down things like that."

"What would you write, then?"

Vance thought the stranger was being a bit intrusive, but he tried to give a straight answer. "Oh, I don't know, other than the usual things like head count on cattle and such. Probably things I needed, like fence staples or kerosene. Shorty keeps one. Why don't you ask him?" Vance had noticed that Em and Shorty didn't seek conversation with one another, so he didn't mind pushing Em off in that direction.

Tip spoke up from where he sat by the fire. "Shorty keeps the names of all the girls he knows. Isn't that right, Shorty?"

"No, not all of 'em. I wouldn't want it to fall into the wrong hands."

Tip played along some more. "Well, what *do* you write in it?"

"Things I don't want to fergit."

"Like what?"

"Whether a stream flows to the right or left. Sometimes I can't remember a detail like that for the life of me."

"But you never write girls' names?"

"Oh, I didn't say I never did. I just said I didn't write 'em all."

With Shorty holding the deer legs up and rocking the body from one side to another as needed, Vance got the carcass of meat separated from the hide. By then it was time to take the horses to water for the night, so he decided to bone the deer in the morning. It was just as well, he thought, to let the meat cool and firm up overnight.

He and Shorty took the horses to the creek and let them drink, three on each side. Shorty stood across the stream from Vance, not much more than a yard away, and spoke in a low voice.

"Those little jokes about the tally book

didn't set well with Fred."

"Oh, really? I didn't notice. I didn't think he was paying any attention."

"He wasn't until we started talking about the girls. Then I could see he was listenin', and he didn't like it."

"What would it matter to him?"

"Oh, he gets so sore about Charlotte."

"Well, that's a problem all by itself." Vance had an image of Charlotte, the blond girl with blunt breasts and crooked teeth. Fred thought she was his girl, but she took a turn with just about everyone else. She didn't do it for the money, as the talk went, but just to get men to want her — and to spite Fred, according to some.

"That it is, but he's touchy about it."

"Oh, does he think she might be one of the names you didn't write down?"

"He might have a pretty good hunch. But the thing is, there's nothin' he can do about it. He can't take it out on anyone in particular, because she's done it with so many. But just the idea that someone else is doin' somethin', it seems to set his pot a-boilin'."

"He won't say anything to you, though."

"Oh, no. Like I said, he can't. But he's got a chip on his shoulder about it, and he'll take it out on someone else if he can."

"Like Em?"

"Or Rusk."

Vance let out a long breath. "So that's part of what's eatin' on him, then, huh?"

"I think so. He's got some kinks in his rope."

"Do you think some of your whorehouse humor has gotten under his skin?"

"Oh, not so much that, I don't think. Most of what goes on in those places is pretty impersonal. But when it's personal — you know, the idea that a woman he wants to have all to himself is givin' herself to someone else — why, that just puts a burr under his tail."

Vance gave it some thought for a moment. Maybe that was part of the reason Fred had gone on about Rusk. What he couldn't do anything about with Charlotte was raising its head somewhere else, and maybe one of the kinks in his rope had to do with Marianne. Maybe Fred couldn't stand the idea of what she'd done.

"Well," Vance said at last, "we're supposed to be in this mess to back up him and Tip over their brother gettin' killed. I didn't throw my hat in because of anything else that happened to Moon, or anything that Fred might think happened to him. It

101

doesn't hurt to remember that. And that goes for anything else Moon might have done."

"I'll go along with you on that. Like I said before, Moon was no saint, and I wasn't surprised that he'd gotten into some kind of trouble."

"He was a natural for it, and it came his way."

"Yes, and if it hadn't been that, it might have been somethin' else. Maybe men kill each other over women, but they do it for money, too. And not to mention any names, but Moon crossed some people. Call 'em A and B. Sooner or later, they'd want some of it back, and they've got a couple of birds they can send to do the job."

"Uh-huh. Like a couple of buzzards on a fence rail."

"Not to mention any names. And not to speak ill of the dead, but I think Rusk just happened to get to him sooner. So you're right. We need to remember what stake we've got in this game. I'm in it to back up Tip, and look out for him if I can. And to hell with anything else."

"That's me, too. I wouldn't have come along if he hadn't convinced me. He wanted a chance to even things up."

"So we try to help him get that chance."

"That sounds about right. And like you say, it doesn't hurt to remind ourselves of that."

When they got the horses watered and staked out for the night, they went back to camp, where the fire had burned down to a faint bed of coals. Vance crouched next to it for the comfort more than for the heat. Fred and Em had already turned in for the evening, but Tip was still up, sitting on his bedroll and looking at the last of the fire.

"Make sure I get up as soon as you do, Tip. I'll cut some steaks for breakfast first thing, and then I'll bone out the rest to take with us. I can do the whole thing in less than an hour."

"That's quite a bit of meat."

"Oh, I won't take every little scrap. I'll get the big pieces off the shoulders, the haunches, and the backstraps. We'll probably eat one side of the backstrap just for breakfast, between the five of us."

Tip nodded as he continued to stare at the dying fire. Vance could tell that tomorrow's breakfast was not the uppermost thing in Tip's mind, and he doubted that Rusk and the Mexican were, either. Vance recalled the sight of a pretty girl with hair the color of wheat straw, standing on the sidewalk and waving.

Vance lay in his bed with his eyes closed, trying to shut out the moonlit sky and go to sleep. Somewhere off in the night he could hear a mourning dove with its haunting *coo-coo-oo*. When he and Shorty had been coming back with the deer at dusk, he had seen the silhouette of a horned owl on the top of the sandstone wall west of camp. The dove's call was stronger than a person remembered, and at first it reminded Vance of the hooting of an owl until he placed it better. The owl might have gone back to the nearest trees by now, the few short ones Vance had seen scattered on the ridge top. Some animals traveled a ways for water in this country, like the deer that had come for his evening drink, while others, like the owl, came to hunt. And here they were, five men and six horses, taking their share. A little stream such as this one would support a lot of life, both the hunters and the hunted.

Vance rolled over, as if he could find a soft spot on the hard ground. Now that he slept in a bed most of the time, he noticed it more when he had to turn in a hard bed. The blankets had not dried out all the way that morning, and he had not thought to roll out his bed when they first set camp, so it had a bit of a musty smell to it. But that was all right. A few nights in the open, even on uncertain business, gave him a distance on things back home.

Someone in camp was snuffle-snoring. Vance hadn't heard the sound the night before, and considering the direction where the sound came from, he thought it might be Em. Vance wondered if the man had anything more than a blanket for his bed. Whatever bed he had, he had laid it out on the other side of Fred's, and Vance hadn't gotten much of a look at it.

That fellow Em was one to be watched. Vance still wasn't sure why he was tagging along to begin with and what kind of nerve he had. He probably had the courage of a coward, which meant he might try to prove he had guts, as he said, but he would do it when he was sure he could pull it off. Now that Vance thought of it, he was glad that Em rode in front with Fred. It was better than having someone like that in back, keeping an eye from there.

The man had a prying way about him, like the business about the tally book. What the hell difference did it make if a fellow had a book, or what he wrote in it?

Some men could keep all the details of a ranch outfit in their heads, while others like to write everything down in ledgers. A tally book was a kind of ledger in miniature, without columns, where a fellow could jot down everything on the same page, such as how many cows had calves, on what date he had had his mare bred, and how much flour he needed to buy. He probably didn't put his deep secrets into writing and carry them around on his chest.

Vance turned over again. There was something he was trying to remember, like trying to place the call of the dove. Then he hit upon it, and it didn't have a thing to do with Em.

Nate Cousins had kept a tally book, and when his friends found him, it was gone. They found him in his cabin, where from the number of bullet holes in the plank walls it looked as if he had held off two or three men for quite a while until they got to him. Dead men couldn't tell stories, but his friends figured he must have gotten a look at whoever was shooting at him and then might have written down their names. They said he died game. People who weren't his friends said he had more calves than he should for the number of mama cows that carried his brand. Those who were his friends mentioned no names — call 'em A and B — but they said a couple of big outfits had taken a dislike to him. So if he had written any names in his little book, they might have been the names of a couple of birds who saw fit to lift the evidence.

They said he died game. He might have been a rustler, but they said he had guts when it came to the end. It was small consolation to Josie, who seemed dead on her feet for a long time after that. She didn't take care of herself, and she shuffled around with a blank, sunken look on her face. Some of it, Vance was sure, was due to the baby she was carrying. It made her heavy and slow. But when the baby was born with darker features than either of them and she named it Ethan, Vance thought he understood. What he had to do was not begrudge the baby, not treat it like just another mouth to feed.

Chapter Six

In the morning, Vance rolled out early and went to work on the deer. By the time Tip had coals for the coffee and skillets, Vance had the backstraps, or loins, trimmed out of both sides of the backbone and had a plate stacked with fifteen little steaks. Each steak was three-quarters of an inch thick and about four inches across the long way. Tip smiled as he took the plate, and within a few minutes the smell of bacon grease and frying meat rose in the morning air.

Now with the daylight a little better, Vance probed inside to take out the tenderloins, which lay inside the ribs and against the backbone on each side. Making careful strokes with the knife, he lifted out two pieces about a foot long and an inch and a half across. Prime breakfast meat.

"These are the best cuts," he said to Tip as he handed him the strips. "We might as well use them up this morning, too. They won't keep quite as well as the rest, anyway."

Vance went back to work, boning out the

hindquarters and then the shoulders. When he was done, he had a heap of neat, clean venison with no bone and little fat. It was forty pounds at the most. The carcass lay on the ground in one large piece consisting of the rib cage and backbone, with the four loose leg bones inside the cavity. Vance had not bothered with the rib meat, figuring he could leave it for the coyotes and for any magpies or crows that might come this way. By the time he got the carcass hauled off and deposited in the sagebrush a good hundred yards from camp, he saw that Shorty was finished with watering the horses. He washed his hands in the creek and returned to camp.

By that time, everyone else was eating. Three steaks waited for him in one skillet while the pieces of tenderloin fried in the other. With his knife he speared the steaks and set them on his tin plate, then sat down to eat.

Shorty offered a compliment on the grub, and Tip and Em agreed. Fred, who didn't seem to like to concede anything, made something like a grunt of agreement. After a pause of a couple of minutes, he spoke.

"We don't want to lose any time gettin' packed and gone."

Tip looked up. "I don't see what's wrong with cookin' up another mess of these steaks and carryin' 'em along for noon dinner."

"We're gettin' a late enough start as it is." Fred sniffed and then lapsed into his sullen mode until he finished the meat on his plate. Then he got up and sauntered off to roll up his bed.

"What's eatin' on him?" asked Shorty.

Tip answered, "He doesn't want to take any of that meat along. Says we've got enough, and it'll just slow us down and probably spoil as well."

"Oh, to hell with him," said Shorty in a matter-of-fact tone as he cut off a bite of steak. "It's good meat, and we can use it. Pack it on top of the camp stuff and underneath the bedrolls, and it'll keep just fine."

"Fred says no."

Vance could feel his anger coming up. "Look," he said. "How about if you put my bedroll on top of the whole pack, and I'll load the meat onto the back of my saddle?"

"Why not?" added Shorty. "If Fred has his bedroll on the packhorse, he can hardly complain about someone else's."

Tip lifted the skillet from the coals. "These are ready. Let's go ahead and clean 'em up." With his knife he pushed five or six pieces onto each of their plates. As he settled back into his place, he said, "I think we can do it that way. Vance, you put your bedroll on the pack, and I'll carry mine."

Vance felt like a mutineer until he told himself it was just a matter of being reasonable. "Thanks, Tip. It sure seems like a petty thing to bicker about."

"I know. Especially when we've got such bigger things to go after."

Vance rolled up his blankets without the canvas ground sheet, saving it to wrap the venison. With Shorty's help he stacked the meat to make a bundle longer than it was wide, then rolled the bundle and tied it. By the time they had their two horses saddled and packed, Fred and Tip were covering the load on the packhorse and tying it off.

As the four of them started to lead the horses out of camp, Shorty looked around and stopped. "Where's Em?" he asked.

Vance turned around, taking in the whole area around the camp. The tagalong was nowhere in sight.

"I don't know," Fred answered. "I thought he was with you two."

Vance looked at the brothers. "I wasn't paying much attention, but I thought he was standing by and watching you two. Looks like he slipped away."

Shorty spoke up. "He's a slick little son of a bitch, I'd say. I think he got away with my watch."

"The hell," said Fred.

"The hell, yes. I noticed it missin' when I was done with the horses, but I didn't want to say anything over breakfast. I just figgered I'd keep my eye on him for a little while and see how he acted before I called him on it outright. Then I got caught up with gettin' things packed, and when I looked around, he was gone."

Fred shook his head. "Doesn't sound right to me. Not for a fella that doesn't like to travel by himself. He'll be sorry if we catch up with him after this."

"If he's even goin' that way." Shorty had his lips tight against his teeth as he studied the ground. "However he got out of here, he didn't leave any tracks on the trail."

Fred turned his stirrup out and put the toe of his left boot into it. "Well, let's get going," he said. "We've got a lot of ground ahead of us if we're goin' to catch those two we're after." When he had swung up into the saddle, he said, "Sorry about your watch, Shorty. For your sake, I hope we catch the little bastard."

They rode out onto the trail at a brisk walk, moved into a trot, and then picked up a lope for about a mile before slowing down to a fast walk again. This was the way to do it, Vance thought. Cover as much ground as possible in the cool of the morning.

As the party moved along, Vance fell into his own thoughts again. Recalling the various pieces of conversation he had had with Shorty, he began to wonder if this mission was the same one he thought he had set out on. Fred's urge to catch up with Rusk and punish him might have more to it than simple revenge for the death of his brother. And the brother, in turn, was seeming less and less like someone worth getting shot over. Vance looked around at the group, taking in each of the others with a brief glance, and then he reminded himself of what he and Shorty had as much as spelled out. They were in it for Tip, not for Fred or Moon or anything that either of them had done. They were backing up Tip in his belief that he deserved a chance to get even. As long as Vance could define that purpose and come back to it, he could keep himself from wondering what the hell he was doing in an expedition led by Fred Dunham, with a sneak like Emerson Prophet worming his way in and then slinking away.

At about an hour into the day's journey, the group came to the top of a hill and saw a herd of sheep down the hill ahead of them, right on the trail. Fred held up his hand, and the group stopped.

"Shall we ride around 'em?" Tip asked.

Shorty answered. "I'd like to ask 'em a couple of questions about who they've seen."

"So would I," Fred added.

Vance looked at the gray mass of animals and picked out a sheepherder on each side of the flock. The one on the far side was leading a pack mule, and the one on the near side was waving to a dog that was running back and forth ahead of him. "They look like Mexicans," he said.

Fred spit off to his right side. "Then a lot of information we'll get out of them."

Vance shaded his eyes against the bright sun as it hung at nine o'clock. "I'll talk to 'em," he said. "I don't mind."

"It's not just that. They won't tell on one of their kind." Fred looked around at the group. "But there's enough of us that they won't give us any trouble."

By the time the party rode to the bottom of the hill, the two sheepherders had let the flock move ahead and were now standing by the trail to face the riders. The man leading the mule stood a couple of steps back from his partner.

Vance held up a hand in greeting and called out, "Good morning," then swung down from the saddle so he wouldn't be looking down on the two men.

Except for a rifle and scabbard strapped onto the pack mule and ready at hand, Vance saw no hint of danger, and as he met the look of each of the two men, he did not sense any hostility. They were both dressed in drab, dusty clothes, and neither of them wore a gun. The man nearest him was about his own age, thirty or so, of average height and build. He had quick eyes and a dark mustache, with a few bristles on his chin. The one who stood back, holding the pack mule, was an inch or two taller. He had a full beard and a pockmarked face above that, and he looked muscular.

"Speak English?" Vance asked.

"Little bit," said the man nearest him.

"Which way are you going?"

The man motioned eastward with his head. "Over there. Takin' the sheep to water."

"I see. Where you comin' from?"

"Over there." The fellow pointed to the northwest.

"Uh-huh. And where do you go when you get the sheep to water? Over the mountains to the river?"

"Oh, no. Too hard. We go back this way." He motioned with his thumb to the southwest.

Vance was able to imagine a sketch of their route. "Had any trouble?"

"Not too much. Little bit."

"Oh. Seen anyone? Like, yesterday or today?"

"Two men."

Vance felt his pulse jump. "Really? Where?"

The sheepherder pointed to the north-northwest. "Over there."

"What kind of men?" Vance hesitated, then added, "One of them a white man?"

"They both white."

"Oh. One of 'em have a beard?" Vance gestured with his thumb and fingers where his own beard would be.

The Mexican shook his head. "No, they both shave."

"Hmm. What do they look like, then?"

The man frowned and looked at nothing in particular, as if searching for the words. "One of 'em, he's pretty white, but not all the same." He moved his fingertips back and forth in front of his cheekbones.

"Kind of splotchy or muddy?"

"Yeah, muddy."

"How about his arms? Did he have the sleeves cut off his shirt?"

The Mexican frowned again and shook his head. "I don't know."

Vance motioned with his right hand along his left sleeve. "Did he have this part of his shirt? Did he have the whole shirt?"

"Oh, yeah. He got the whole shirt."

"Could be him anyway." Then, in a more deliberate voice, Vance said, "How about the other man? What does he look like?"

The sheepherder drew his thumb and fingertips together in front of his right eye. "He got eyes that stick out."

"Bug eyes? Like a frog?"

"Yeah. Like a frog."

Vance looked at Shorty. "You know who that sounds like?"

"Sounds like Short Sleeves and Bug-Eyes, two buzzards on a rail." Shorty turned to Fred, who had a questioning look on his face. "Winslow and Ludington."

Fred's face gave a twitch downward, but he didn't say anything.

Vance looked at the Mexican again. "Did those two men give you some trouble?"

"Just a little bit. They say they don't like

us and they don't like sheep."

"Ah, they don't like anybody. Was that all they did?"

"They make sure we see their guns."

"Of course. But nothing else?"

A shake of the head. "No."

"You didn't see a man by himself — alone?"

Another shake of the head.

"And you didn't see a man with a beard?" Vance motioned with his hand again. "Maybe riding with a Mexican?"

"No. Just those two."

"Well, I guess that's about it. Thanks for tellin' us what you've seen." Then, as an afterthought, he said, "How are you fixed for meat?"

The man shrugged. "Oh, in a stew."

Vance reconsidered. "What I mean is, do you have meat? To eat?"

"No, we don't kill nothin'. No sheep. And we sure don't kill no cows."

"Do you want some meat?"

The man shrugged again. "I don't know."

"Look. I killed a deer." Vance patted the bundle on the back of his horse. "I got a lot of meat. I'll give you some."

The man turned and spoke in Spanish to his partner, who answered in the affirmative. "Sure," said the first man.

Vance looked at Shorty, who swung down from his horse and helped untie the pack. Vance unrolled it on the ground and lifted out the two hunks of shoulder meat.

"Here," he said. "I just killed him last night. Nice young one."

The Mexican gave the meat an approving look, nodded, and then met Vance's eyes. "Thank you."

"My pleasure. We've still got plenty." Vance pointed at the bundle on the ground and then bent over to roll it up again, with Shorty's help.

The sheepherders' dog, a black-and-brown mix, had come near and was sniffing the air. The man who had spoken to Vance uttered a few syllables at the dog, and it moved away.

When Vance and Shorty had the bundle tied back onto the horse, Vance saw that the sheepherders had taken out a cloth sack and had wrapped their fresh meat in it. An amiable mood hung in the air as Vance and Shorty mounted up.

Vance touched the brim of his hat. "Thanks, amigos, and good luck."

"Thank you," said the one who had done the talking. "I hope you find what you're lookin' for."

As the horsemen turned to ride away, Vance heard both Mexicans say, "Que les vaya bien." *We hope it all goes well for you.*

"Gracias," he answered.

When the party had ridden past the sheep and down the trail a quarter of a mile, Fred spoke. "I thought that once you'd given 'em the meat, you might have gotten a better answer out of 'em."

Vance looked at Fred and then off to the northwest. "They weren't anywhere near this trail when Rusk and the Mexican would've ridden through here. And they didn't mind telling us about the two they did see."

"Huh! Those two."

"Sounds just like 'em, too," said Shorty. "Got nothin' better to do than push around a couple of Mexican sheepherders on foot."

Fred sniffed. "As far as that goes, I don't like sheep either, and I don't care all that much for Mexicans. And there's one that, if I catch him, had better be sayin' his prayers."

"I'm not surprised they haven't seen the Prophet, either," Shorty put in. "I haven't seen his tracks at all."

They rode on through the morning as the sun rose in the sky, warming the air and the ground. Whenever the men stopped and dismounted, Vance could feel the heat coming up from the soil. When they were moving, always at a fast walk at least, the five horses raised a cloud of dust that hung in the air for a while before it settled. From time to time, Vance turned in the saddle to watch the backtrail and to scan the country around them. The air was hazy with all the particles that accumulated in late summer. The land looked bleak and barren and scorched as it rolled away in the distance, with grass that was sparse and brittle — hospitable to few cattle, Vance noticed. Now and again the riders would raise antelope, sometimes a lone buck and sometimes a small band ranging from three or four to six or seven.

Vance thought about the sheep they had seen earlier in the morning. That bunch would be well behind them by now, maybe still strung out along the little creek, foraging along the edges and dipping a hundred gray muzzles in the narrow stream. A fellow never knew what was upstream from him when he drank or washed from a creek, and Vance was glad to know that the sheep had been headed toward the water and not on their way back from an overnight stay.

It gave him a good feeling to know that the sheep were behind, and he was also satisfied just to know where they were. He couldn't know for certain where anything else was roaming in this hard land. Rusk and the Mexican, by all evidence, were pushing ahead on the trail. Winslow and Ludington might be nosing around off to the west or to the northwest or even straight north, in back of the four riders. And Emerson Prophet, now something of a fugitive, was drifting somewhere out in that huge triangle of land between Medicine Bow in the north, Elk Mountain in the south, and Rawlins in the west.

At about noon, Shorty took the group off the main trail to the west. "Tracks lead this way," he said. "Comin' and goin'."

Half a mile away, they came to a tiny trickle of water, not much more than a seep, flowing north. Fifty yards downstream, someone had dug out a hole for the water to collect in. As Shorty looked over the situation and nodded, Fred spoke.

"Looks like they camped here."

"Sure does," Shorty answered as he got down from his horse.

"Last night, or the night before?"

Shorty crouched on the ground where someone had scratched out a little fire pit and tended a fire. Shorty put his hand over the ashes. "Night before last, I'd say. This little squaw fire went cold a long time ago, and the mud around that hole is dry and cracked." He looked at Fred. "That means they're still over a day ahead of us."

"That's hard to believe."

"Well, we don't know how fast they're movin'. That is, we know from the tracks that they're not runnin' their horses to death, but we don't know how early they hit the trail or how long they push it each day. They were a little over a day ahead of us yesterday in Medicine Bow, and if they camped here the night before last, it would have been a long ride but they could have made it. I think it's more likely that they gained a little on us than that we closed the gap so much that they camped here last night. Especially with the ashes that cold and the water hole the way it looks."

Fred scowled. "And there we were, like schoolkids on a holiday, off huntin' deer and whatnot. We should have rode further."

Shorty scratched at the dirt with the toe of his boot. "We camped where we found water. If they had come through much later, they might have camped in the same place as we did, but it still would have been a day ahead."

"I just don't like it."

"None of us do." Shorty gave a shrug as he looked up and around at the others, who were still mounted, and then at Fred again. "But I don't want to fool myself into thinkin' we've gained on them. It just doesn't look like it."

"Well, let's ride, then." Fred gathered his reins.

Shorty gave him a patient look. "We should at least water the horses while we can. There's enough in that hole for each horse to drink about a half gallon or so."

Tip got down from his horse. "Good idea. I can dig out four cans of tomatoes, and we can eat 'em in the time it takes to water the horses."

Vance dismounted and held his horse, Tip's, and the packhorse while Shorty took Fred's horse and his own to water. Fred walked around the little campsite, kicking at the ground.

"I'd like to find one thing that I could be sure came from them. Not for proof — I know it's them that's been here — but I'd just like to have some little thing that they left."

Tip looked over his shoulder as he dug into the pack. "They're travelin' light and not wastin' any time. It's not like a wagon train that throws something out every hundred yards and carves their names on rocks."

Fred gave a hard look through the dull sheen of sweat on his face. "They're travelin' lighter than we are, that's for sure. And that Mexican probably wouldn't know how to write his name anyway."

"You never know who can read or write," Vance said. "Not on the basis of how much you dislike him."

"That's right," Fred allowed. "Even Shorty keeps a tally book." Then, with a quick emendation he said, "Not that I dislike him, of course."

Ah-hah, Vance thought. Shorty was right about Charlotte.

"Four cans," said Tip, straightening up from having reached in and rummaged around in the pack. "Don't miss Em at all."

The sun did not budge during the short midday stop. It still hung straight overhead when they rode back onto the trail. They moved at a trot, raising a cloud of dust that hung in the air for a while as Vance looked at the backtrail.

Less than an hour into the afternoon, Shorty said they had lost the trail.

"What do you mean?" asked Fred.

"What I mean is, they quit puttin' down tracks on the main trail. They didn't just up and fly over them peaks there, but they done somethin'. And we need to circle around to find out what it was."

"All of us?" asked Tip, looking back at the packhorse.

"No, we don't need all of us," Shorty answered. "Me 'n' Fred can ride out, and you two can wait here. Save the horses a little."

Vance and Tip got down from their horses and watched as Fred and Shorty rode back on the trail they had just traveled. Shorty turned his horse and headed west with Fred following. Half a mile out, they stopped and rode around in a circle, then headed farther west for another half mile, then turned south. A few minutes later, they turned and rode back to join Vance and Tip, who mounted up again.

"It looks like they took a detour," Shorty announced. "I think they rode around and planned to catch this same trail again farther ahead."

Fred spoke next. "That may be. But we didn't follow the trail all the way out. They could just as well have doubled around in back of us."

"What makes you think that?" Tip asked.

"I seen dust. Shorty did, too."

Vance and Tip both looked at Shorty.

"Someone's back there," he said. "Just no tellin' who, from this distance."

Chapter Seven

The four riders had all turned their horses to face north. Vance could see a faint rise of dust, not quite thick enough to be called a cloud, that wiped away and vanished.

Fred squinted with a hard-set look to his face. "They must have stopped. It's not rising any more. Maybe they seen us stop and then did the same."

"You think it's them?" Vance asked.

Still giving a hard look, Fred nodded.

"It might be someone else," Vance went on. "I doubt that Rusk and the Mexican would have circled around and lost a day, just to come up from behind. If they were a day ahead of us, which seems like the case, how would they even know we were back here? If there's someone in back of us, it's most likely someone else."

Fred spit, then motioned northwest with his head. "I don't care if it's the two we're followin' or if it's someone else. I don't like to be followed, and I want to find out who it is."

"I'll stay here and mind things," Tip offered, "if you two want to go look." He dismounted.

Fred turned to Shorty and gave a curt nod. The two of them set out on the backtrail.

Vance got down from his horse and held its reins along with the reins of Tip's horse and the lead rope of the packhorse. Tip went about fiddling with the lashes and tightening them a little.

"Loosened up a bit when I was diggin' out the tomatoes," he said.

"Uh-huh." Vance watched Fred and Shorty riding north, taking it at a slow pace, he imagined, so as not to raise dust themselves. When they got to the base of a high rise in the land, both riders got down. Shorty stayed with the horses as Fred made a slow climb to the crest of the hill. He took off his hat, paused for a moment, and then came scurrying down the hill. He and Shorty mounted up and came back to the rest of the group, once again keeping their horses to a slow walk.

Vance and Tip mounted up and faced the other two riders.

"I think it's them," Fred reported when he was close enough not to speak in a loud voice.

"Rusk and the Mexican?" asked Tip.

"It was too far away to put a beard on the one fella. But I'm sure the other one was the Mexican."

Tip cocked his head. "What were they doin'?"

"They just pulled off the trail and was makin' a stop in the shade of some rocks."

"Damn little shade," remarked Shorty.

Fred let the comment pass and then said, "Let's go back and make 'em face up to us."

Vance didn't care for Fred's impetuous tone. "Why didn't you get a better look through the binoculars?"

"I didn't think of 'em till I was already up the hill, and I didn't want to waste time comin' back for 'em."

Vance raised his eyebrows. "But we'll take time ridin' back now, when we don't know for sure."

Fred exploded. "Damn it! I think it's Rusk and the Mexican, but I don't care who it is. We'll find out what the hell they're doin' behind us."

Tip spoke again. "Are they right on the other side of that hill?"

"No, there's another one, lower, a ways back, and they're on the other side of it, next to some rocks." Fred had a calm expression on his face as he looked around at the other three men. "They're stopped and not expectin' anything. I say we just ride into their camp and ask what they're doin', and then take it from there."

Tip shrugged. "Might as well."

Shorty glanced at Tip and then Vance. "I suppose so."

Vance, who sensed some hesitation on Shorty's part, didn't like the plan himself but couldn't see where his opinion mattered. As he adjusted his reins, he said, "I suppose so, too."

Fred set out first, his horse taking off at a regular walk. "Let's not raise too much dust," he said. "The less they expect, the better, but there's more of us no matter what."

When the party topped the first rise, Vance expected to see something beyond the next hill, but he didn't. That might be all right, he thought. If his group couldn't see the camp, then whoever was there might not be able to see the riders coming toward them. Wherever they were, they had moved since Fred's sighting.

Down the riders went and up the next hill, making very little noise. Then, when they cleared the top, Vance could see the other party's camp. It sat off the trail, a hundred yards this side of the rocks. Vance could see three horses, stripped and pick-eted, and two men, neither of whom had a beard or looked like a Mexican. The two men, he could see well enough, were Winslow and Ludington.

It was too late to turn back. Vance could see no good coming out of this encounter, but they were going to have to go through with it at this point.

Fred spoke in a low voice. "Let's ride side by side, four across."

Tip moved to Fred's left side and Vance moved to Shorty's right. As they moved down the hill, Vance thought Fred was making a foolish show of force at a point where all they were doing was saving face.

Winslow and Ludington got up from lounging on the ground and stood a couple of yards apart with their camp behind them. Vance noticed that Winslow, who stood at Ludington's right, was wearing a long-sleeved shirt, just as the sheepherders had mentioned.

A movement farther back caught Vance's eye. A person stepped out from behind the rocks and walked toward the camp. That accounted for the third horse, he thought. Then he saw who the man was. It was Em-erson Prophet.

"Well, I'll be damned," said Shorty in a

low voice. "I wonder if he was in cahoots with them all along, just come to do a little spyin' on us."

"I don't know," said Vance. "But I don't like the looks of it."

As the group came to the bottom of the hill, Fred called out a greeting. Winslow called back and the riders went in, stopping about ten yards from the other men.

Fred dismounted and the others followed suit. Regardless of what these others were up to, it was their camp, and if the riders weren't passing through, common courtesy called for them to dismount and not to look down on the others as they all talked.

Ludington spoke first. "Well, what brings you fellas out this way?"

Fred answered, "I could ask you the same thing."

"Well, we're just mindin' our own business, out checkin' on cattle." As the man smiled, Vance could see his bug eyes taking in everybody in the group.

Fred motioned with his head toward Em, who had come up behind Ludington and now stood a few paces to his left. "Is this your apprentice?"

"Might be, but why don't you answer my question first? You come ridin' into our camp, and you apparently put yourself out to do it, so it's a reasonable question for me to ask. What are you-all doin' out this way?"

Fred scowled in the direction of Emerson Prophet. "As if you didn't already know. But I can tell you straight, no bones about it." Fred looked to his left and then to his right, to take in his company. "We're after a man named Rusk and a Mexican that's runnin' with him. The two of 'em killed our brother Moon in Rock River, which I imagine you heard about, and we aim to catch up with 'em."

Winslow spoke now. "Aren't you goin' the wrong way, then?"

Fred turned to face him. "Maybe for a minute, but I wanted to know who was followin' us."

"Little Bo Peep," said Ludington.

Vance caught an antagonistic note in Ludington's voice, and he wondered if the man was making fun of Fred, of the brother he had lost, or of the sheepherders.

"You can make all the smart remarks you want," Fred answered, "but we're on serious business, and I thought it was worth our while to double back."

Winslow spoke again, showing yellow teeth. "Did you think we were the ones that got your brother?"

Vance recognized the tactic now. He hadn't seen Winslow and Ludington use it before, but he had heard how they liked to work a fellow, passing him back and forth. It didn't seem as if Fred, for all his sense of his own command, knew he was being drawn in. Vance thought of putting in a comment himself, just to change the flow, but he decided to stay back and let Fred do as he wished.

"If you mean, did I think it might be those other two back here, then yes. It looked like they'd done some circlin' around a ways back, and if they was in back, I didn't want to miss the chance."

Winslow's brown eyes flickered away from Fred and then back to him. "You boys seem pretty eager to get those two."

"The sons of bitches killed my brother Moon, and if I can, I'm gonna make 'em pay."

Ludington's voice came up again. "Maybe they had cause."

"What do you mean?"

The bug eyes looked calm as Ludington settled his gaze on Fred. "Your brother Moon was a tinhorn. Everybody knew it. It's no surprise someone got him."

Time seemed to stand still. Winslow,

with his light, blotchy complexion, and Ludington, with the dull shine of old sweat on his face, were both looking at Fred. His face had gone heavy, and Vance wondered if he was searching for an answer or just measuring what he was up against. Then he spoke.

"I don't care if they had cause. When someone does your family a wrong, you don't just sit and take it. You do somethin' about it."

Ludington answered, "You and how many others? You come ridin' into our camp like you thought you was an army."

Fred's face quickened as if his blood came back up. "They jumped my brother two to one. If we're bringin' along a couple of others, that's just a little insurance to keep things in our favor."

Vance expected Winslow to speak again, but Ludington answered.

"I hope you find 'em," he said with a tone of self-assurance that made Vance think the man knew something, but it was anybody's guess what it might be.

Fred's confidence, or perhaps his natural tendency to meet another man's bluff, took over. "We will," he said. "We damn sure will."

The atmosphere among the men seemed

to relax. Fred shifted his feet, and Tip glanced at the packhorse. Vance became aware again of the reins in his own left hand, and he waited for another word or phrase to signal an end to the meeting.

Shorty cleared his throat and then spoke. "Before we go, I'd like to mention somethin'."

Vance felt a ripple of worry come back up. It didn't seem as if they were going to get out that easily.

"What's that?" asked Winslow, who was farthest from Shorty.

"I'm missin' somethin'."

"Just a couple of inches of height," said Ludington. "I wouldn't worry about it, little cowboy."

Shorty ignored them both and kept his eyes on Em. "I think you might know what I'm talkin' about."

The weasel face lifted. "I'm sure I don't."

Half a minute hung in the air as Shorty wet his lips and bored his gaze on Emerson Prophet. "Well, I suppose these fellas know you was travelin' with us until this mornin', and for all I know, you might've been their apprentice before that. However or why-ever you slipped in on us, I don't know. But when you slip out the way you did, you make people wonder. Especially when there's somethin' missin'."

Em glanced at his two companions and then, with something close to a sneer, he said, "Why don't you make sense?"

"Maybe I will. Maybe I'll be a little more pertickler."

"Go ahead."

"I had a watch, and it turned up missin' this mornin'."

"Well, if it turned up lost after I'd left, you can hardly say I took it."

"No, I saw it was gone before you was."

"Then you should have said something."

"I thought I had plenty of time. I didn't know you was goin' to leave so quick." Shorty raised his eyebrows. " 'Course, I didn't know we'd run into you again so soon, either, but since we did, I thought I'd mention it."

"Well, you did," said Ludington.

Shorty looked at him and then back at Em. "Now, how about it?"

"How about what?"

"My watch."

Em's voice took on an insolent tone in the company of his two protectors. "Well, what about it? If you can't take care of your things, what do I have to do with it?"

Shorty's voice was hard as iron. "I'm

tellin' you, I think it was taken. I didn't lose it. So why don't you just out with it, and we'll be done with it."

"Just out with it," Em taunted.

"That's right. Give it back."

"You're sayin' you think I took it."

"Yessir, I am."

Winslow spoke up. "You know, little man, you're bringin' trouble into our camp."

Shorty glanced his way. "It was here already. I don't know how long you've known this fella and I don't care. But once I was here, I thought I'd see about gittin' back somethin' that disappeared when he did."

Ludington chipped in, "Well, he says he doesn't know anything about it."

"I think he does, and I don't think it would take much to prove it."

Ludington came right back. "You think, you don't think. Well, I'll tell you what. Don't think you can come into our camp and start pushin' around, thinkin' you're goin' to find something."

Shorty's eyebrows went up again. "My quarrel is with this fella here." Then, looking at Em, he said, "If you just gave it back, that would be the easiest."

"You're saying I took your watch."

"That's right. We've already been through it."

"You're callin' me a thief."

"If the shoe fits —"

Em turned to his left to spit, then said, "Why, you little son of a —" Before he had turned all the way back to face Shorty, he was pulling his gun.

Vance jumped to the right to stay out of the line of fire. From the corner of his eye he saw Shorty come up with his six-gun and fire before Em could get off a shot. Em turned back and to his right, dropping his pistol. As he staggered backwards, another shot roared.

Shorty fell back against his horse and the animal pulled away, squealing, as Shorty hit the ground. The others held onto their horses as they lurched and reared; then when things settled down, Vance could see Ludington as he stood with a six-shooter at waist level, still at the ready in case anyone else came in on the fray. Beyond him, Winslow had drawn his gun and had the Dunham brothers covered.

Shorty looked up at Vance with pain in his eyes. "Git my horse for me, please."

No one showed an inclination to shoot anymore. Em, the one who had pulled the first gun, was lying on the ground and holding his right arm with his left. Satisfied that no one was going to shoot him in the back, Vance swung onto his horse and went after Shorty's. The animal was trotting south along the trail, and when Vance caught up with it, he saw a red stain on the horse's chest in front of the left shoulder.

He grabbed the loose reins and turned the horse around, then headed back toward the other men. It had happened all in a moment, and now they had Shorty and his horse both hurt. Vance decided not to say anything about the horse until they all got clear of the hostile camp.

Winslow and Ludington both had their six-guns back in their holsters, as did Shorty, who knelt on the ground and held his blood-covered left hand against his abdomen. Em was sitting up now, still holding his right arm. His holster was empty, and his pistol lay on the ground a few paces in front of him.

Vance got down to hold his own horse and Shorty's as Fred helped their wounded comrade crawl up onto the saddle. Then Fred, Vance, and Tip all mounted up. Vance had the impression that no one but Shorty had said anything since the gunfire broke out, and as he separated his reins from Shorty's, he wondered who would speak first.

"It's too bad things like this have to happen," said Ludington. "But you fellas came into our camp, and whether you were lookin' for trouble or not, you got it."

Fred glared in Em's direction. "It was that little son of a bitch pulled his gun first."

"He was goaded into it," Ludington answered, "and after that, there was one shot on each side. Could've been more. Best thing to do is call it even. Count yourselves lucky it didn't come to more than it did."

Vance, still holding both pairs of reins, turned to Shorty and saw a pale, blank face. He was sure the little puncher was hurt worse than the weasel who had started the gun-pulling. But they were going to have to call it even unless they wanted to ask for more trouble. "Hang onto your saddle horn, Shorty," he said, and nudged his horse toward the trail. As he looked around to see Fred and Tip falling in behind, he heard Winslow call out a parting taunt.

"And don't come back."

No one said anything as the group rode south again over the first rise and then the next. Shorty was hunched over his saddle horn and still hanging on, but he didn't look good. His horse was lagging, and Vance could tell from the way Fred and Tip looked at it that they knew it had caught the bullet that went through Shorty.

Less than a mile south of the scene of the fight, Shorty fell out of his saddle and spilled onto the ground. As Vance knelt by his side, he felt sick at the sight of his friend's shirt and vest soaked with blood.

Shorty took small wheezing breaths with his mouth open. "I'm no good," he said. "I'm not gonna make it."

Vance knew he was just talking as he said, "C'mon, Shorty. Try to hang on a little longer."

Shorty moved his head back and forth slowly. "Nah, I'm done for. I can tell. It was that other son of a bitch that shot me, wasn't it?"

"Yeah, it was him. Ludington. Prophet never got a shot."

"I didn't think so, but it all happened just like that." Shorty took a couple of labored, open-mouthed breaths. "I just can't get enough air," he said.

Vance looked up at Fred and Tip, who stood by their horses. "Let's see if we can give him a little shade." Then, with his hand on Shorty's arm, he said, "Hang on, now. No one's in a hurry. Just take one breath after another."

Shorty gave a weak smile and shook his head. "No, it's no use." After a couple more breaths he said, "He didn't even shoot, did he?"

"No, he didn't." Vance thought, what a thing to get killed for, but he said nothing.

Shorty closed his eyes and then opened them. "Vance?"

"Yeah, Shorty?"

"I want to ask you —" Shorty cocked his head as he took a few deliberate breaths, still with his mouth open.

"Go ahead, Shorty. What do you want to ask? Something you want me to do?"

"Yeah."

Vance expected Shorty to ask him to get even with Em, and he was wondering how he would answer. "Go ahead. I'm listenin'."

"Look after Tip, would you? Don't let the same thing happen to him, would you?"

"You bet, Shorty." Vance looked up and saw Fred and Tip, both gazing off to the west as if they had heard nothing. He looked back at Shorty, who was smiling.

"Good pals."

"That's right, Shorty. We all are." Vance waited as Shorty took a few more breaths and seemed to be trying to focus. "Something else, Shorty?"

"More pretty girls."

"You want more, or there are more?"

"Yep."

"I'm not sure I followed you, Shorty. You say there's more pretty girls?"

Shorty smiled. "Uh-huh. More pretty girls than one."

Shorty's horse died an hour after he did. Fred was minding the horses as Tip and Vance scratched out a grave in the dry, hard soil. According to Fred, the horse was standing up alive one minute and keeled over dead the next. As Tip and Vance continued working on the grave, Fred took the bridle and saddle off the dead horse. Then he took Shorty's outfit, including his bedroll, rifle, and six-gun, to hang in a tree about a mile to the east.

"We can get it on the way back," he said.

Vance could not find it in himself to care about his dead friend's outfit. All he could think of, over and over again, was that Shorty had died for no good reason and that he, Vance, had not done enough to try to keep the others from doing something

145

that he thought was a bad idea. Maybe he wouldn't have changed the outcome, but at least he would have done something. But he hadn't, and now he was scratching at the ground with a rock, repeating to himself, "I'm sorry."

As they finished the work and made ready to set out on the trail again, Vance thought of how he had closed things with Shorty. *Good pals*. Well, they were that, even if he hadn't done better. *Look after Tip*. He would try to do that, but with Shorty gone, things were more out of balance than before. *More pretty girls than one*. Maybe that was the one thing Vance could feel all right about. Without mentioning it to anyone, he had made sure that Shorty's tally book had gone to the grave with him, safe in the inside pocket of a blood-stained vest, protected by a pair of crossed hands that would never throw a rope again.

Chapter Eight

There had been a time when he thought he would like to kill Nate Cousins, indeed. Looking back, Vance could see it was only an idea, just a fancy thought of something he would never have done. If he had it in him to kill anyone at all, it should have been someone who deserved it — someone like Winslow or Ludington. But that was one of the big troubles in the world: the crooked sons of bitches that ought to be killed were too often the ones that didn't get it.

Kill someone. That would take a hell of a lot more than anything he had shown in the last while. As he went back through all the events that led up to the shooting, he couldn't pick a moment at which he might have done something that would have kept Shorty from getting into the fight, but he could think of several times when he had done nothing at all. He had gone along on this ill-advised quest because of Tip and Shorty, and even when Fred had had one wrong-headed notion after another, Vance had left it to Shorty to do most of the disagreeing. To begin with, he had thought of Shorty as the balance to keep things reasonable between the two brothers and the two friends, and Shorty had done his part. Vance had not, and now Shorty was dead.

Vance could think back and recall several instances of Fred being thick-headed. Riding into Winslow and Ludington's camp was the most obvious, but even with the stupidity of Fred's insisting he had seen the Mexican, Vance could not put all the blame on Fred. He himself had gone along rather than hold out for something sensible when he knew better and had said as much, and once they were in the other men's camp, Fred had not done anything to start the shooting. At a moment when they could have ridden away, Shorty braced Em on the question of the watch and wasn't cowed by the other two. He had more guts than Fred, but his dislike of Em got him into trouble on his own. That was how Vance saw it. Fred brought them into the camp, just as he had gotten them to go on the chase to begin with, but he didn't push the fight that ended Shorty's life. Shorty did that on his own, and Vance had just stood there, jumping out of the way when the bullets flew.

Vance gave a slow nod as he rode along

in silence. Fred had done too much, and he himself hadn't done enough. Everyone had a share in the blame — except maybe Tip. Vance took a sidelong glance at the youngest Dunham brother. He seemed innocent, a boy who was getting too far away from his sweetheart, and yet he had gone whole hog with Fred on this idea of getting even. *Look after Tip*. Vance knew there was honor in keeping his word to a dying friend, but he also knew that a smart man would be thinking about just pulling out and going home. Still he rode on, thinking of the reasons that kept him here. There was Shorty's request, along with Vance's initial agreement to stay on for four days. Then there was the matter of putting a good face on things. He wouldn't show much courage if he pulled out as soon as someone got killed. Even if it were the smart thing to do, it wouldn't wear well.

Vance fell back on a few words to help explain to himself why he was still on this expedition. *Look after Tip*. He wondered if he could. He had done a damn poor job with Shorty, but Shorty would have been quick to say he didn't need anyone to look after him, and maybe Tip needed it more. He wasn't as tough as Shorty, and he didn't seem to be aware of how much he fell under the influence of his brother. As Vance thought about it, another image appeared — a pretty girl standing on the sidewalk in Rock River and looking on with hope and worry. That was part of it, too. If Vance was supposed to look after Tip, which he imagined meant protecting him against Fred as well as against Rusk and the Mexican, then he imagined he was supposed to protect Ruth against those things as well.

On they rode, through the later afternoon and early evening. As the heat of the day began to wear off, they saw what looked like trees and a canyon up ahead.

"It's about time we came to the river," Vance offered. "That might be it up there."

The trail crossed the river in the bottom of a small canyon, not far from a ranch house that looked inhabited. Fred rode into the yard but could not raise anybody, so the party crossed the river and then stopped to water the horses. Vance admired the clear, rushing water and the small, round rocks on the shoals. Crouching upstream from the horses, he washed his face and drank from the cool water. It was a refreshing stop after the long, parching ride from Medicine Bow.

The trail rose up to higher ground and followed along the left side of the river, which ran along a broad canyon reaching a few miles to the southwest. Dark green trees rose in clusters along the watercourse, with green grass in the open spaces. Here and there Vance saw what looked like hay meadows. This little valley might get snowed in during the winter, he thought, and it might be chock full of mosquitoes in the summer, but it was a restful sight at the moment.

They made camp in a stand of cottonwoods about fifty yards from the river. As Vance strung out a picket line for the horses, it occurred to him that it would have been handy to keep Shorty's rope for a time like this, when there were trees and a fellow could tie a line from one to another. Once he had the line set up, he took the horses two at a time to drink from the river. Again he washed his face in the cool, rippling water. The Medicine Bow River looked more like a mountain stream here, where it splashed over polished rocks, than it did farther north, where it flowed across the plains. He had to remind himself it was the same river they had camped on when they first set out only two days earlier.

Two days. It seemed as if much more time than that had passed, and now that he was by himself with the two Dunham brothers, it seemed as if the party had been reduced by much more than one person. Shorty left a big empty spot — not only in humor, which would be in short supply from now on, but in competence and cool-headedness. As long as Shorty had been riding along, Vance had not questioned his own reasons for going with the Dunham brothers. Now with Shorty gone and the new pattern setting in, he wondered how much it had to do with being friends with Tip and Shorty, and how much he had been swayed by the idea that a man had a right to try to get even. As he thought back, he realized that idea might have had more persuasion a couple of days earlier than it did now.

Vance finished watering the horses and set them out to graze. As he walked toward the blaze of the campfire, he noticed that dusk was settling into the long shadows of the canyon. He wondered if Winslow and Ludington were still following, as it seemed they had been doing at least for a while if not longer, and he wondered what reasons they had. If they wanted a quarrel with Fred and Tip, they had just passed up an opportunity. Vance had the sense that their tailing the Dunham party had something to do with Moon, as hinted by Shorty in his references to A and B, but the reasons remained hazy.

Casting his thoughts in the other direction, he tried to imagine Rusk and the Mexican somewhere out on the trail. They must have gotten even farther ahead today even if, as Shorty had said, they were not traveling fast. Tomorrow would be the fourth day on this chase, and Vance had his doubts as to whether he would ever see Rusk or the Mexican in the flesh. For the present, they drifted in the distance as imaginary figures.

Back at camp, Fred had come up from the river with a canvas bucket of water and was hanging it on the stub of a low-hanging cottonwood branch. Tip had the remnants of the first side of bacon sputtering in a skillet as he sliced steaks from the deer loin. Fred smiled at Vance, showing his yellow teeth, and crossed the campsite to take a seat on his bedroll.

Vance sat on the ground nearby and leaned back against his bedroll. "Long day," he said. "How much do you think they gained on us?"

Fred shook his head. "Oh, maybe a little.

But we can make up some of our time tomorrow."

"They could be quite a ways ahead by now."

"I don't give a damn if they gained a little, 'cause we'll get it back." Fred swelled up as he took in an audible breath through his nose. "I know we're goin' to catch up with 'em, and like I said before, when you know you're in the right, you've got the edge."

Vance thought Fred had some brave talk after what had happened earlier in the day, but he just said, "We'll see."

Tip looked up from laying steaks in the skillet. "See what?"

Vance shrugged. "We'll see if we even catch 'em."

Tip gave him a square look. "We will."

Vance wondered at Tip's sudden answer. Something in the tone of it gave him the impression that Tip, who like himself had not done anything to keep Shorty from getting killed, was now willing to redirect his resentment toward Rusk and the Mexican, as if there were now more cause than before to run them down.

Fred seemed to be pleased by his brother's assertiveness. With a look of satisfaction spread across his face, he said,

"You're damn right we will."

Then he reached back for his duffel bag as Vance had seen him do before. After rummaging around for a moment, he brought out his strange little object, the thing Tip referred to as a lucky charm. Fred rubbed his thumb across it a couple of times, then released it and came up with a bag of Bull Durham. He maintained silence as he rolled the cigarette, licked and tapped the seam, and lit the end. Then, with his air of authority, he spoke again.

"No adulterer and no Mexican is goin' to get away with what they done. And that's it."

Vance reflected that Rusk would have to be married himself in order to be an adulterer, but he didn't think the distinction was worth making with Fred. The camp fell into silence, except for the sizzling of the steaks, until Fred finished his smoke. He stood up, took a couple of steps toward the fire, and flicked the cigarette stub into the coals.

Tip, who had just turned the steaks, sat back on a low, wide river rock. "You've got to wonder what that tagalong Em was doing in that other camp."

Fred scratched his jaw and yawned. "Probably the same thing he was doin' with us. Moochin'."

From all the moments of conversation since the incident with Winslow and Ludington, Vance had formed the impression that Fred didn't want to talk about it. But he, Vance, wasn't going to pretend it hadn't happened. So he spoke up.

"I think he had something to do with them before he fell in with us, and then when he could give a report on what we were doing, he went back to them."

Fred lifted his head and made a scowl. "Maybe he did, and maybe he just goes from one place to another lookin' for a tit to suck. But I can't worry about him, or them other two either. They're not after us, or they would have done something when they had a chance. As far as I'm concerned, I'd rather worry about who's out ahead of us than who's behind."

"That wouldn't have been a bad way to think earlier in the day," Vance said. "Shorty might still be alive."

Fred turned to loom over Vance and glower at him. "That's easy to say now. Me 'n' Shorty was followin' a hunch, and it turned out different. But once we got there, Shorty picked that fight for himself. He should have been more careful."

Vance felt the anger mounting, but he

156

told himself not to do anything rash. As well as he could remember, the hunch to which Fred referred had been Fred's alone, but there was no way to argue the point. Nor could he disagree that Shorty should have been more careful. But it burned him to hear Fred simplify things that way with what seemed to be a mixture of ingratitude and petty spite. Somewhere at the bottom of it all, Vance imagined, at least part of Fred's lack of sympathy could be traced back to his resentment about a woman. Then, to give Fred his due, Vance considered how Fred might have acted if it had been Vance himself who had been killed. He supposed Fred would still have been an ingrate with someone who had never lifted Charlotte's skirt.

As Fred turned and went back to sit on his bedroll, Vance got an off-guard look at him. Beneath it all, he thought, a strange kind of selfishness drove the man. Fred could sound righteous about his brother getting killed, and in so doing, he made it seem as if he took it more as something that happened to him than as something that happened to Moon. The same tone seemed to resonate when he harped about Rusk, the man who had touched another man's wife. Fred made it sound like something that had been done to him. Reacting to things on such a self-centered level had no doubt helped him to deflect Shorty's death as if it were something in which he had no blame. He could leave it behind him.

Vance didn't like letting Fred have the last word on Shorty, but for an answer, the only terms he could think of were blunt — Shorty would never have come near Emerson Prophet, either the first time or the second, if he hadn't been helping Fred carry out his own selfish vendetta. On the one hand, Vance was tempted to put the argument in those terms but, on the other hand, he knew that if he did, he would jeopardize whatever civility they needed to maintain among themselves. So he buried his resentment for the time being and looked for something cheerful to say.

"How's the grub comin', Tip?"

"Just fine. Blood's comin' up on this side."

Supper got under way with the clacking of knives on tin plates. Fred had a nonchalant air about him, as if always being right were something he could wear lightly. Vance felt himself getting irritated again, and after a few minutes he formed a question.

"I'll tell you, Fred, I've given it some thought, and I can't figure it out."

"What's that?"

"How in the hell did you look down into their camp and think you saw the Mexican?"

Fred's face turned stolid in the firelight. "It was quite a ways off."

"I realize that, and I understand that you didn't want to take the time to go back and fetch your field glasses, but what I mean is, which one did you think was him? Ludington doesn't look like a Mexican, and Winslow even less."

Fred didn't answer right away. A sullen expression crept into his face, and after his characteristic delay, he said, "I know what I thought I saw."

Vance wanted to say that Fred saw what he wanted to see, but he thought that would be too antagonistic. It would be better, he thought, to get Fred to admit he had made a mistake.

A sound from the darkness cut off their conversation. It was a voice, a man hallooing the camp.

In a loud voice, Fred called him in.

Vance looked at Tip and said, "It probably wouldn't hurt to get back from the firelight."

The two of them set down their plates, stood up, and stepped back into the shadows. Fred set down his plate, went to his saddle where it lay on the ground, and pulled his rifle from its scabbard. Then he stood at the edge of the light.

The sound of hoofbeats, one horse walking, carried on the cool night air. "Comin' in," said the voice. Then a shape emerged from the darkness.

Vance saw the white blaze on a horse's forehead, then four white socks, and then a man in drab clothes walking next to the horse.

"Evenin'," Fred called out.

"Good evenin'," answered the man in a gravelly voice that was cheerful all the same. "Don't mean to bother you for long."

"No bother at all," answered Fred. "Come on into the light."

The man stepped forward, as did the horse. Vance could see it was a well-kept, well-groomed animal, meant to make a good impression. The white blaze and socks made a sharp contrast with the dark, blackish brown color of the rest of the horse. The man himself was less impressive, being shorter than average and having a common, almost low-class appearance.

He had squat features, including low brows, an upturned nose, wide lips, and ears that stuck out. His clothes were nondescript and had seen quite a bit of use since their last washing.

As the man and horse stepped into view, Vance and Tip did the same.

"Name's Nanno," said the stranger. "Joe Nanno. Everyone calls me Joe."

"Good enough," Fred answered. "I'm Fred Dunham." He looked around and, seeing the other two in the firelight, he said, "This is my brother Tip, and this is our friend, Vance Coolidge."

Joe glanced at each man and nodded. "Well, like I said, I don't plan to stay long. I just thought I'd check with you fellas to be sure of where I am."

Fred smiled, showing his teeth in the firelight. "Where do you think you are?"

"Along the Medicine Bow River, north of Elk Mountain."

"Well, that's where we are."

"Mighty fine," said Joe, looking around and smiling as his words hung on the air.

Tip glanced at the ground, where his plate was, and then said, "We were just sittin' down to eat. You're welcome to join us."

"Oh, no," the man answered in a not

very convincing tone. "I wouldn't want to put you to any trouble."

"No trouble. We've got plenty of deer meat, and I can fry you up a couple of steaks in no time."

"Oh, I don't know —"

"Don't be shy," Fred cut in. "Make yourself comfortable, and if you don't mind watchin' us in the meanwhile, Tip'll have yours in a few minutes."

"Go ahead and eat. Don't let your grub get cold on account of me. I can't be in any hurry, not if I'm traveling in the dark."

Vance spoke up. "I've got a picket line strung out over there. If you want, you can tie your horse to it."

"Not necessary. He's trained to stay right where I drop his reins. Stand there all night, till I tell him otherwise."

"Uh-huh," Fred interjected. "Good-enough-looking horse."

"He's not bad." Joe led the animal to the edge of the light, dropped the reins to ground-hitch him, and came back to the fire as the others were sitting down. At Fred's invitation he took a seat.

"So," Fred went on, "you're on your way somewhere tonight?"

"That's right." Joe's eyebrows went up as Tip put the skillet on the fire. Then, turning his gaze on Fred, he said, "I'm plannin' to stop at a ranch up here a ways, where the trail crosses the river."

Fred nodded as he poked a bite of steak into his mouth. Then, speaking around the food as he chewed it, he said, "A couple of miles back. There wasn't no one around when we came by, but there might be someone there now."

"Not hard to find, then?"

"Not at all. Just stay on the trail. If your horse can follow the trail in what moon-light we've got, you should get there all right."

"No trouble with that," came the answer. "He's a good 'un."

Fred glanced at the horse again. "Looks like it." Then, holding a chunk of steak on the tip of his knife, he looked at the visitor and said, "You a horse trader?"

"I consider myself more of a horse buyer." Joe's voice, in spite of being grav-elly, had a smooth, assuring tone to it.

"Oh, you go around and buy top horses, then?"

"I do." Joe drew out a bag of makings and went to work on a cigarette as he talked. "I buy well-trained ranch horses."

"I see. But you must sell 'em — unless you buy 'em for someone else."

Joe smiled, and his jug-ears seemed to stand out more as his whole face lifted. "Oh, I do that part, too. I sell 'em. But the important part is findin' 'em and buyin' 'em."

"Of course," Fred answered. "You don't just buy and sell any old horse."

"No, not the common run of horseflesh, though there's plenty of men who do that, and some of 'em make an honest living at it, and a good one." Joe smiled again, and Vance noted his ruddy complexion. Then Joe's face relaxed and his eyebrows went up again as Tip laid three loin steaks in the hot skillet.

"Everyone's gotta make a livin'," Fred went on, "and there's lots of ways of doin' it."

"There sure are."

"Now us, we're cattlemen."

Joe looked around and nodded, as if he were going along with something for the sake of politeness.

"We run our own places over by Rock River. We're on personal business right now."

"Oh, uh-huh." Joe tossed his head back and then forward in emphatic agreement.

Fred gave a thoughtful twist to his mouth. "But you know, a man can't help thinkin' once in a while whether there's other ways of makin' it."

"Oh, there sure are. As many as you can count."

"Just in the horse business itself, there's horse raisin', and trainin', and buyin' and sellin'."

"You bet. And roundin' up stray horses, too. There's money in that. More than in wild horses. You go out and hunt horses that strayed on the winter range, or whatever. Horses with brands, that people want back."

"Have you done some of that?" Fred asked.

"Oh, a little. Mostly I buy good ranch horses. But whatever I do, I work with horses that I can get good clean papers on."

"No reason to do it any other way."

"That's for sure. You're right about that. Like I was sayin' to a man and his wife that I met a while back, honest work lets a fella sleep good at night." Joe turned his gaze toward Tip. "That's startin' to smell pretty good. You must be a good cook."

Tip smiled. "Just try to keep from burnin' everything."

"Deer meat, you say?"

"That's right. Vance shot it just yesterday."

Joe smiled at Vance. "Well, I'd better give my thanks to you, too. You must be a good shot."

"I try not to miss."

Joe glanced at his horse and then turned back to Fred. "You've got a couple of good straight-up boys here. What did you say your last name was?"

"Dunham. We're cattlemen."

"Sure. Just hadn't heard the name before."

"If you get up around Medicine Bow and over toward Rock River, you will."

"Oh, I'm sure."

As the conversation went on in the same fashion, Vance wondered at the light nature of it all. Fred never mentioned the reason they were traveling, nor did he mention his brother Moon, much less Shorty. Two men were dead, two men were meandering on the backtrail, and two men were out ahead somewhere. Fred would love to get either Rusk or the Mexican in his sights before the sun set again, but here he was, swapping commonplaces with a man who described himself as a horse buyer. Then, in the middle of a discussion of how much money could be made in the hide-and-leather business, Fred dropped in a question.

"Seen a white man and a Mexican travelin' together?"

"Nope, sure haven't." Joe was eating his steak by now, and he stared at his plate for a few seconds. Shaking his head, he said, "No, nothin' in that area at all."

"The white man's name is Rusk. Don't know about the Mexican's."

Joe shook his head again. "I don't always catch names, and I don't believe I've heard that one of late." Then, as if in afterthought, he said, "I asked you your name because you'd already said it, and because you were settin' me up so good."

Vance remembered that earlier moment, and he remembered thinking that the fellow might be something other than a horse dealer. "Say, Joe," he said.

"What's that?"

"How much is that horse of yours worth?"

"That one?"

"Yeah."

The gravelly voice came out smooth and practiced. "Oh, he's a good horse. Good-lookin', smart, and got a heart of gold. I'd take five hundred dollars for him."

Vance nodded. "I bet he's worth it."

Joe smiled, and his face lifted. "He sure is, boy."

★ ★ ★

When Joe had gathered up his reins and gone on his way, the other three sat in silence for a few minutes until Vance spoke.

"Well, I think he's a sure-enough horse trader."

"Oh, yeah," said Fred, reaching into his duffel bag and pulling out a bottle. "I was wonderin' how long he was gonna stay."

"He didn't seem to have seen Rusk and the Mexican," Tip remarked.

"Naw," said Fred as he squeaked open the bottle. "But that don't mean nothin'. We'll get 'em."

Chapter Nine

In the morning as he was taking the horses to water, Vance noticed a cut on the front left foot of the packhorse. The wound, which appeared to be a few days old, was on the back of the foot between the fetlock and the hoof, in the area Vance had learned to call the pastern. Facing the rear of the horse and standing with his left hip next to the horse's leg, Vance bent over and picked up the foot. The cut opened, revealing a pale interior that was starting to get slimy. Vance let the foot down. A cut like that wasn't going to get better by itself.

He tied the horse to the picket line and watered the other two. It was the kind of wound that a horse picked up from barbed wire, getting his foot stuck in the wire and then jerking away in panic. It might well have happened on the night of the hailstorm, and it was in a spot that didn't meet the eye most of the time. Shorty had been taking this horse to water and Tip had been in charge of the pack, and neither of them had noticed. Vance himself hadn't seen it the evening before. Most riders checked their horses' feet from time to time as a matter of habit, but no one had been paying close enough attention to this one.

On his way back to camp, Vance caught a whiff of frying bacon. When he got closer, he saw that Tip was cooking a mess of it for breakfast. Fred had his bedroll tied up and was sitting on it, smoking a cigarette. Vance looked at the skillet and saw the thin black smoke lifting above the curled bacon and sputtering grease.

"I think I might have a use for some of that grease," he said.

Fred took the cigarette from his mouth and blew out a stream of smoke. "What for?"

"That packhorse has a cut on the back of his front left foot, just above the hoof. It's about a quarter of an inch deep and goes clear across. Look like it's startin' to get infected. We can let the bacon grease harden up a little, and I can pack some of it in there. It'll keep dirt from gettin' in, and the salt'll draw out some of the fluid."

"That'll work," said Fred, as if he were approving a request. "I've done it myself."

Tip spoke. "What do you think got to him?"

"Looks like something he might have picked up the night they all got scattered in the storm."

"Well," Fred cut in, "you can smear some grease on him, and he'll be all right."

"I think we might want to do a little more than that," Vance said.

"Like what?"

"Keep the weight off him, or at least lighten it."

Fred gave a disapproving look. "What the hell? He's the packhorse. And he hasn't been limpin' any that I've noticed."

"No, not yet. But if it doesn't get tended to, it could turn into a limp that might not go away."

"Ah, hell."

"I think we should take some of the weight off him, shift it around to the other horses."

Fred scowled again. "I told you we were carryin' too much weight."

"We're carryin' less all the time. By my count, we've got three cans of tomatoes left, and we can eat those at noon. They weigh the most, except for the skillets."

"I'm talkin' about the deer meat. I'd pitch it out."

Vance felt his anger rising, and he warned himself. "There's less of that all

171

the time, too. We've eaten two full meals out of it, including the horse trader, and I gave some to the sheepherders. We've got a small piece of loin left and the two hindquarters — the best parts. I'll cut the shanks off and toss them out. That'll be a few pounds."

"I'd throw out the whole damn thing."

Vance looked at him squarely. "Maybe you would, but I'm not going to. I'll pack the deer meat, my own bedroll, and a skillet. If each of you packs your own bedroll and a little more, it'll go lighter on the packhorse and he'll stand a better chance of knittin' up the way he should."

"Sounds all right to me," said Tip. "What do you want me to do with the grease? Put it in a can?"

"No, I think it'll cool better in a broader area. Let's leave it in the skillet for right now. After we eat, I can try coolin' the bottom of the pan in the river."

Fred stood up and snapped his cigarette butt into the fire. "Lotta work," he said. "But you boys do what you want, and we'll see what the hell time of day we get out of here."

After breakfast, Vance took the skillet to the river and, holding it by the handle, rested it on a couple of rocks in a shallow.

After a while the cast iron cooled and the grease turned opaque. Vance dragged his finger through it, feeling the grains of bacon on the bottom of the skillet. The grease was still runny, not yet firm the way he'd have liked it, but usable all the same. He picked up the skillet and carried it to the picket line where he had left the horse.

Leaning as he had done before, he set the skillet on the ground on his right and picked up the horse's foot with his left. The cut opened again, and the sight of it made him glad he had decided to do something about it. Lifting a gob of grease with the first two fingers of his right hand, he smeared the creamy paste into the wound.

Then came a surprise. The horse kicked with his rear hoof and struck Vance on the forearm. Vance dropped the front foot and straightened up. As a general rule, a horse couldn't kick if he had a front leg raised, but the sting of the bacon grease in the open wound must have been sharp enough to make him stand on two feet long enough to get in a quick kick. Vance rubbed his forearm. With whatever support he had given by holding up the front foot, he had helped himself get kicked. Good enough, he thought. The animal would be better for it.

Fred and Tip had their horses saddled with the bedrolls tied on, and they had the camp outfit bundled up as well. Vance handed them the packhorse and went to work saddling his own. When he had that done, he took out his knife, cut off the shanks of the deer meat, and tossed them into the underbrush. He didn't like to waste even that much meat, but he reminded himself that he was doing his part in the compromise.

When he had his load tied on, Fred and Tip were ready to go. All three mounted up, and after a look around, they moved out of the clearing. The morning sun had not yet cleared the bare mountains to the east, so everything still lay in half shadow. Vance, who had fallen in line behind the others, took another look as he put the campsite behind. There at the edge of the trees, beneath a clump of sagebrush, lay an empty whiskey bottle. Vance imagined it was Fred's, as he hadn't seen it earlier when he was coming and going with the horses, and he tended to keep an eye on the ground when he was on foot.

They followed the trail along the river, heading south and west toward a notch in the landscape. It looked as if the little valley closed and the canyon ended there,

174

and beyond that the country opened up. The morning being cool, the riders moved at a fast, steady walk for a couple of hours as the sun rose at their backs. Every once in a while, Vance looked back to see how the packhorse was traveling. It was moving fine, with nothing irregular in its gait.

At mid-morning the party came to the spot where the valley and canyon ended and the country changed. Several miles to the south, Elk Mountain loomed above the surrounding hills and ridges and rolling plains, all of which had more green and looked more hospitable than the country through which they had ridden from Medicine Bow until the spot where the trail crossed the river. Greenest of all this new panorama was Elk Mountain, with sloped meadows reaching up to patches of dark timber. Across the plain, from the base of the mountain to the mouth of the canyon, trees and lower-lying greenery marked the courses of the river and whatever forks or creeks fed into it.

The men continued to follow the trail, which ran more or less parallel with the river. More than once they rode within a quarter mile of antelope, bright tan and white against the green background, and the area looked to Vance like a good place to jump deer in the morning and evening and maybe a good place for elk when the winter drove them off the mountain.

As the sun rose toward its daily zenith, the men rode easily across the plain toward Elk Mountain. Vance wondered, as he did from time to time, whether they would catch the men they were following. Fred seemed confident that his party was still on the same trail, and Vance found himself not caring. If Fred got them onto the wrong trail and lost another half day or more, then the game was up for Vance and he could go home. If they were still on the right trail and by chance caught up with the other party, then they would be doing what they set out to do.

At a little before noon, Vance noticed a gang of magpies about a quarter mile west of the trail. The birds were lifting, lighting, and squabbling over something in the grass. Vance mentioned it to the others, and the three of them decided to ride over and have a look. As they rode closer, the magpies rose and flew away in their various directions. The men had to ride to within ten yards of the scene, where the grass was matted down, to tell for sure what was there.

The magpies' feast was hosted by the

remnants of an antelope hunt, as Vance saw from the hides and heads that lay off to one side. Someone had killed a doe antelope and a young buck. Looking at the carcasses themselves, he thought something was out of order. One hulk lay propped lengthwise against the other. The legs had been cut away from both, so the carcasses were oblong objects. As Vance looked closer, he could see that the animals had not been gutted. He had not seen this method before, but he could reconstruct how the hunter or hunters had done things, first skinning the animals and then severing the shoulders, separating the hind legs at the socket joints, and carving out the backstraps. Whoever had done it had plundered the biggest pieces and left the rest, mainly rib and flank meat but also the tenderloins inside. The carcasses had begun to dry and turn dull, except where the bird pecks had opened up white specks of fat and tendon.

"Looks like something that happened yesterday," he said.

"Probably Rusk and the Mexican," Fred asserted. "They'd have needed grub by now."

Vance began to notice more bird pecks all along the flesh that had stayed on the spine. "I don't know," he said. "I don't see why they'd go to the trouble of killing and butchering two. Whoever did this made quick work of it, but it would still be twice as much as those fellas needed to bother with."

"Oh, I bet it was them," Fred answered. "The time is just right."

Vance shrugged as he looked at the spoiling remains. He couldn't decide whether it looked like greedy work or just laziness. He had heard of and seen the work of meat hunters who exploited just the best cuts, sometimes with nothing more subtle than a hatchet, but he hadn't felt as he did now. Something about the condition of the carcasses — the lack of dignity as much as the waste — bothered him. He shook his head. It didn't matter. It was someone else's business, someone else's leavings. He climbed back into the saddle and the party set off again toward Elk Mountain.

A mile or so later, they stopped for the midday rest. First they watered the horses, then squatted in the shade of a young cottonwood as they ate the last three cans of tomatoes.

Vance saw clouds beginning to pile up in the west. "Looks like we might be in for some rain," he said.

Fred cast a glance over his shoulder. "I doubt it'll rain much."

Vance did not give an answer. As time wore on, he was forming the impression that Fred's disagreement was almost automatic, as if any expression of opinion contained a challenge to his authority. Maybe that was why Fred clung to his wrongheaded ideas once he forced the evidence to fit his notions — he did not like to admit he was wrong, and he did not like to allow anyone else to be right.

Not far from the base of Elk Mountain, the trail made a turn to the west. Up ahead, as Vance understood it, the trail ran through Rattlesnake Pass and then came out on the plains to the north and east of the little town of Warm Springs. Having been to the mountains south of here and having looked out onto the plains from there, he had a general picture of the layout of the country. The low mountains or high hills up ahead, larger than what he would call foothills, resembled the country he had seen farther south. But Rattlesnake Pass itself he did not know, much less what they might find there.

As the gathering clouds blocked out the sun and cooled the afternoon, the three riders made good time. Elk Mountain lay directly on their left as they rode parallel to its lower reaches. At one point where the trail straightened out after curving down into a low spot, Fred pointed at a cluster of buildings that huddled against the hillside on their left. It looked like some kind of way station, with a broad, squat cabin for the main building, a couple of sheds or stables that must have been built at different times and did not match, and a set of pole corrals. All of the lumber and rails had a weathered hue that looked even duller in the cloudy afternoon.

Two horses in the front corral, along with smoke threading from the chimney of the cabin, showed signs of habitation. Vance decided to put his thought in the form of a question so that Fred would have less of a compulsion to disagree.

"Do you think we should stop?"

"Wouldn't hurt. We can ask if they've seen anyone come by." Fred pointed his horse toward the buildings and gave a touch of the spur.

As the party rode up to the station, the front door of the cabin opened and a man stepped out. Hatless, he had a full head of dark brown hair but no beard or mustache. He was a good-sized fellow, about six feet tall and tending toward heaviness. Closer now, Vance could see that the man held his head up as if he were appraising the company, and the dark brows and prominent cheekbones gave him a cold, almost arrogant look.

"How do you do?" he called out.

"Not too bad," Fred answered, bringing his horse to a stop.

Tip and Vance, who had slowed down sooner, came to a rest behind Fred.

"You ought to pile off for a few minutes," said the man. "Rest your horses for a bit."

"Don't want to waste too much time, but thought we'd stop and say hello."

"You bet." The stationmaster gave an assuring smile and nod. "You might think about whether you need anything. I've got quite a few things on hand — grub, ammunition, snakebite medicine."

"Tobacco?"

"Got some of that, too, as it so happens."

"Oh, we might stop in for a few minutes, then." Fred swung down from his horse, then introduced himself and the others as they dismounted.

"Name's Gregory," said the host. "Wynn Gregory. Folks call me Wynn."

Fred gave a short laugh as he shook the man's hand. "Oh, you like to win, then?"

The man laughed back in the same way. "I sure don't like to lose." He looked around at the others. "If you boys want to water the horses now, there's the trough. You can tie 'em at the rail here or put 'em in a corral. Suit yourself."

A movement at the cabin door caught Vance's eye. A woman with mouse-colored hair had appeared. Her eyes met Vance's for a second and moved on.

"Anything I can do?" came the voice.

Wynn looked halfway over his shoulder. "Go ahead and git up some coffee, and I'll see if these gentlemen want to eat." As the woman disappeared, Wynn turned to Fred. "She can cook up a mess of antelope. I've got plenty."

Fred turned down his mouth and moved his head back and forth. "Oh, I don't know. We'll probably eat later on."

"Easier here. I tell you, I've got plenty. I just killed a couple of 'em yesterday, and the meat doesn't keep that long. Not antelope."

Vance narrowed his gaze at the man. "Oh, did you get 'em back over that way, about three miles or so? We saw where someone had killed a couple."

182

Wynn nodded. "Probably mine, but not quite that far, as the crow flies." He turned to Fred again. "Well, come on in."

When Vance and Tip had watered and tied up the horses, they went inside to join the others. Once his eyes adjusted to the darkness, Vance saw that the front part of the cabin was set up like an inn or tavern, with two plank tables in the middle of the room and a bar along the west side beneath a set of elk antlers. Fred and Wynn were seated at the table closest to the bar and had settled in with a bottle of whiskey and two glasses. Each of them had also gotten a cigarette rolled and lit, and they were in the middle of a conversation.

"Not anybody by that description," said the host. " 'Course, I don't care for Mexicans to begin with, but if one of 'em stopped and needed somethin', I'd sell it to him. Not many of 'em come by this way, but if they do, I notice 'em and keep an eye on 'em. Same with niggers and Indians, you know."

Fred nodded as he blew smoke out through his nostrils. "Thievin' bastards, for sure. And this one must have posters out for him somewhere, because he stays out of sight. The bearded fella, if he goes into a public place, tends to go by himself."

Wynn screwed up his mouth and shook his head. "Haven't seen him here." Then he raised his glance toward Tip and Vance. "Sit down, boys. I'll get the little woman busy at dinner, and you can have a drink in the meanwhile." Then he called out over his shoulder, "Hey, we need a couple more glasses."

As Tip and Vance took their seats, Mrs. Gregory appeared with two more glasses and set them on the table. As she brushed past him, Vance thought he caught a murky glance from her, and he could feel the presence of a woman.

Wynn gave her a cold stare. "These boys say they'll eat some of that meat, so why don't you cook up a feed of it?"

Vance looked at Fred and could tell he had accepted the invitation. Vance wondered if Fred had agreed to eat antelope as a way of disregarding their own meat supply, or if he had just wanted to lengthen the visit for the sake of the snakebite medicine. Whatever the case, Fred was in no hurry at this moment.

"Which meat?" As she spoke, Vance saw that she had a gap between her two front teeth, but the teeth themselves were white and even.

"The antelope. The stuff I brought in yesterday."

"Oh. Uh-huh."

As the woman moved away, Vance made himself not look at her figure. Then he recalled the horse trader's reference to having talked to a man and wife, and he wondered if this was the couple.

"Have you had many travelers the last couple of days?" he asked.

Wynn sat up straight and elevated his elbow to take a drag on his cigarette. "None," he said, then squinted as he took in the smoke. After exhaling, he added, "You fellas are the first in three days."

As Vance observed the flushed face, he thought the man looked swollen and uncomfortable even as he tried to look relaxed. "Oh," he said.

Fred joined in. "No one came by while you were out hunting?"

"Nah," said the host, with his air of authority. "I can see this place for the first mile or so, the way I went, and I could tell when I got back that no one had been by."

Vance recalled the woman's furtive eyes. This fellow must keep a close watch on her. "Huh," he said. "We met a horse trader yesterday evenin', and he said something or other about having met a man and his wife."

Wynn's eyebrows rose as he lifted his stubbled chin and shook his head. "Not here. Like I told your boss, there hasn't been anybody come by here." He motioned with his hand at the whiskey bottle. "Go ahead. Pour yourselves a drink."

Vance and Tip poured half a glass each and settled into silence as Fred and Wynn resumed their conversation. After the two had impressed upon one another that they could take care of any man, white or otherwise, with fists alone, they moved on to other topics. Vance did not pay them much mind, but he noticed they dwelt for a while on the prospects of making money at this venture and that. Wynn said there was a pile of money to be made wherever there was a town going up, and Vance wondered why the man was wasting his talents out here on a less-traveled road. Maybe he could keep a better eye on his wife that way, but there were probably other reasons. Vance thought Wynn was the type who might have tried his hand at making money and had to lay out for a while, shooting a mess of free meat from time to time and waiting to see if he was going to turn a few dollars on it or have to throw it out. Between that and selling a bit of ammunition, tobacco, and snakebite medicine, the fellow seemed to be getting by as he talked to travelers about the good money to be made elsewhere.

Vance finished his drink, then got up and said he was going to go out and check the horses.

The clouds had thickened and the day had become more gloomy, but it was still bright after the dark interior of the cabin. Vance went to the packhorse and lifted the foot he had doctored that morning. The cut had not opened or bled; rather, it was covered with a dirty seam where dust had settled on the bacon grease. That was not so bad.

Standing among the horses, Vance felt more at ease than he had felt inside. He wondered how long they would lay over, and he wondered if Fred was taking up this time so that it would look more incidental when he bought a bottle of whiskey for the trail, or if he was pumping Wynn for whatever information he thought he might be able to get out of him, or if he was just sharing opinions with someone who saw the world as he did. Whatever the case, Fred was in good company for the moment, and Vance didn't mind being alone with the horses.

As he looked out across the landscape, he thought of Shorty and felt a pang that his friend would never see any of this again. Shorty, the brave and cheerful cowpuncher who could ride with the best, was lying on his back with dirt in his face. He should have lived longer, to hear the voices of saloon girls and the clinking of coins, to feel the wind in his face as he rode the open country. Vance recalled vignettes of riding with Shorty back when they worked for wages together. They would bring in the horse herd, with Shorty riding out front and the loose horses following all in a gallop as Shorty led them, hooves drumming, into a corral where they bunched and milled as Vance rode in from the drag and closed the gate. He could see Shorty smiling through the dust and commotion, just as he did when they were working a herd at roundup time — Shorty fingering the coils of his rope and shaking out a loop, catching a calf and bailing off his horse. No one thought about the past or the future at a moment like that. A fellow just lived it, took the high spots with the low, swung in the saddle and sang songs, ate dust and washed it down with brackish water. Then all of a sudden one man's life was snuffed out for no good reason, and a fellow like Fred would act as if nothing had happened. Sit around and talk about money that none of them was going to make.

Vance heard the scuff of the cabin door opening. He turned, half hoping to see Mrs. Gregory but not surprised to see Tip.

"Everything all right?"

"Oh, sure. I just thought I'd take in some fresh air as I checked the horses."

"You look like there's something bothering you."

"Nah, nothin'."

"It's not that fellow in there, is it?"

"Oh, no."

"Well, there must be something."

Vance hesitated. "I guess there is." He looked away at the distant hills as he felt the tightening in his throat. "It's hard to say, but . . . I can't help thinking about Shorty." He looked back at Tip. "It just doesn't seem right, that he's gone just like that."

Tip nodded. "It's too bad."

"It just doesn't seem right," Vance said again. "He's gone, and for no good reason."

Tip moved his head up and down in a faint motion. "No, it's not right. But he should have been more careful."

Vance felt as if time stopped for a second. Tip was echoing Fred again — and about Shorty, of all things. Vance just shook his head.

Silence hung in the air for half a minute until Tip spoke. "Anyway, I came out to tell you that the grub's ready. The sooner we eat, the sooner we can try to get Fred out of here."

Vance looked at the sky as he kept himself from saying anything bitter. "Yeah, and there's no tellin' what the weather's goin' to do."

Chapter Ten

The rain started coming down when the men were halfway through their meal. At Wynn's suggestion, Vance and Tip went out and put the horses in the stable closest to the cabin. Then they went in and finished their meal as the rain pattered on the roof, first a light, steady rain and then a heavier downpour, drumming for a good ten minutes until it let up. Mrs. Gregory, who had been sweeping the hearth at the edge of Vance's vision, served coffee and cleared the dishes as Fred and Wynn rolled cigarettes and lit them.

Vance went to the door and looked out. The rain had quit falling and sunlight was breaking through from the west. "Looks like it's passed over," he said.

Tip got up from the table. "We can bring the horses around, then."

"Go ahead," said Fred. "I'll be out in a minute."

Vance and Tip waited outside with the horses for longer than a minute until Fred emerged, carrying what looked like two bottles, each wrapped in newspaper. He stuffed one package into each saddlebag, then swung aboard. Vance wondered if Mrs. Gregory would appear again, but she didn't.

Half a mile out on the trail, Vance rode alongside Fred to ask a question. "When was the last time you actually saw their tracks?"

"Oh, I think it was when we turned west."

"Well, after this rain, we're not going to pick up any tracks from before."

Fred's voice was casual as he said, "Oh, I'm sure they headed this way."

Tip spoke up. "You know, this fellow Wynn says they didn't come by here."

Vance smiled. "I think he meant they didn't ride right past his place. But if they rode wide around it, they could've avoided being seen."

"Could be," Tip answered. "And for all that, you don't know if he's on the square."

Fred yawned. "Who, Wynn? He's all right, and he's got no reason to lie. Even if he met Rusk by himself, he wouldn't cover for him anymore when he found out he was runnin' with a Mexican."

Vance appreciated the logic of Fred's comment and let it slide into silence as he glanced at the country around him. Off to his left he saw three mounds rising out of the plains, dark in their own shadows, and then they slipped from his view. He looked at the country ahead, with ridges cutting across from northeast to southwest as Elk Mountain tapered down in a long, dark slope to the west. From there the foothills met the ridges, and Vance imagined that the pass went between the two formations. The sky was clearing out, and the rises in the landscape cast long shadows eastward. The air was clear and sharp after the rain, and the horse hooves made soft thuds in the earth.

As the trail took them westward toward the pass and the country began to narrow, Vance had to look up to see the ridge on his right. It didn't have many trees, just some along the top and a few here and there in a cleft. Off to the left he saw rock formations like little razorbacks, and then the land again took on the appearance of foothills.

In the first part of the pass, he saw steep hillsides on the left, thick with sagebrush and dotted with cedars. Two antelope, a buck and a doe, sat on a hillside in the late-day sun and watched the party go by. Farther ahead, as the trail went down into the first bottom, a patch of aspens sat motionless on the left.

The riders found a creek and stopped to water the horses. Vance noticed that Fred's eyelids drooped and his face looked dull, and he figured Fred must have tried to make the most out of their stop at Wynn Gregory's station. Fred took out his tobacco and papers to roll a cigarette, which he usually didn't do at times like this. No one spoke as he rolled the smoke, lit it, and blew away a cloud of smoke.

"No tellin' how many times this trail goes up and down," said Vance, "but I imagine at some points we'll be a ways from water."

"I imagine," Fred answered, casting his glance around as if he were always on the watch.

Vance looked at Tip. "So I'd say we'd better keep an eye out, and as we get a little closer to nightfall, we look for a place to camp. If we're gonna catch 'em at all, I think it would be better to do it tomorrow, in daylight. As far as that goes, I think we'll either catch 'em tomorrow or not at all."

Tip looked at Fred. "That's pretty much the way I see it. I wish we'd made better time, but if we push it tomorrow, we'll either do it or we won't."

Smoke curled out of Fred's nose as he spoke. "We'll git 'em. And that Mexican had just better hope I don't cut his balls off."

Vance looked away to keep the others from seeing him roll his eyes. The conversation with Gregory, along with the snakebite medicine, must have inflated Fred's courage.

"At any rate," said Tip, "we'd best be on the lookout for a camp in the next hour or so."

When Fred was finished with his cigarette, the three of them mounted up and rode on. The air was cooling with the onset of evening, and the horses seemed to be holding up fine as they climbed the grade. From time to time, Vance caught a glance of the packhorse, and it was still moving steadily.

Up the next hill and down, they came near the creek again. The hill ahead looked like a long one, and there was no telling whether the country got rougher or easier from here. With the light fading and the air getting cooler, the men decided to make camp.

As usual, Vance took care of the horses while Fred and Tip set camp. The three of them agreed not to bother with supper,

having eaten a heavy meal in the afternoon, but Tip had a fire going and the
blackened coffee pot sitting at the edge
when Vance came back to camp. Tip was
seated by the fire with his arms around his
knees, and Fred was lying on top of his
bed with his hat over his eyes.

Vance squatted by the fire and appreciated the warmth. "Fred's going to get a
chill," he offered.

"He said he was just gonna rest for a few
minutes and then he'd come to the fire."

"Whatever suits him, but it looked to me
like he got a lot of liquor in him. And this
air's a bit chilly for your summer blood."

"I'll go see." Tip pushed himself up and
away from the fire and walked over to the
spot where Fred had laid out his bedroll.

Vance could hear the voices but did not
try to pick up the words. In the firelight he
saw Tip crouched next to Fred, and from
the tone of the conversation he imagined
Tip was trying to talk Fred into getting
covered up. After a little while, Tip came
back to the fire.

"He's covered up. He'll be all right."

"That's good. I think it's going to be a
cold night, in comparison."

"Feels like it."

"I think I'll set out that deer meat to let

it get some of the benefit."

"Good idea." After a minute of silence, Tip spoke again. "What do you think, Vance? Do you think we'll catch 'em, or do you think we've lost too much time?"

"Depends on how they're travelin'. To tell you the truth, I haven't seen enough to get an idea of who these two really are."

"Well, none of us has seen 'em."

"I know. But what I mean is, we haven't seen enough of their leavin's. You can get an idea of a man by the way he leaves things. Like those antelope carcasses, just for an example. I didn't know who left them there, but I had some kind of a notion of the type of person who would have done things that way. And when we met Gregory, it all matched. Now you take this fellow Rusk — we've got a name for him and that's about it. For the Mexican we've got even less. But if we saw more of what they left behind — sardine cans, for example, or tailor-made cigarette stubs, or if we saw where they didn't cover up their messes — well, then we'd have at least some kind of a sense that we knew 'em. And then, in a roundabout way, I'd have more to go on as far as whether I thought we'd catch 'em or not. That's a long answer, but the short of it is, I don't know what to think."

"I think we'll catch 'em."

"And cut off the Mexican's balls?"

Tip laughed. "That was just the whiskey talkin', I think."

In the morning, Tip got up a fire, put on the coffee pot, and rendered some bacon grease as Vance cut some steaks. Not knowing how much longer the trip was going to last, and noticing some discoloration on the outside of the deer quarters, he sliced three large steaks from the middle of one of the haunches. After trimming off the fat and a few rough scraps, he handed the meat to Tip, who had poured the excess grease into a can for the horse's foot. Right away the steaks were sizzling, and breakfast was on the air.

Vance took the horses to water and set them out to graze a little longer. When he got back to camp, Fred was up and about. He looked as if the sleep had done him some good, as he was clear-eyed and alert. When grub was ready he ate his steak without disparaging it, drank his coffee, and then rolled his after-meal cigarette. After that he helped Tip roll up the camp as Vance doctored the packhorse and brought all four animals to camp.

Daylight had not come into the canyon, and the low-lying air still carried a chill when the group set out on the trail once again. The horses picked up a brisk walk, snorting and snuffling as the four sets of hooves clip-clopped on the grade. Vance felt the strength of his chest and arms as he tensed against the cool air.

He thought about Josie, back at their little ranch house on the plains. It seemed a world away from this chase he had been on, where thoughts ran so narrow and resentment seemed normal. In spite of their troubles, he and Josie had been civil to one another, and even if their trust had been damaged, it was in better shape than what he had seen at the Gregory hearth.

He hadn't been able to place it before, but that seemed to be the problem with Wynn and the missus. Neither of them trusted the other. Mrs. Gregory was not likely to ride away with the first man who would take the risk, or even with the first man who could put her husband in his place, but at some level in her feelings she wanted out. That was what the furtive glances seemed to say. Maybe her getting out was confined to an escapade every few years, but she was on the lookout. Vance could tell that much.

It didn't seem to be the case with Josie. Doing something once did not mean she was looking for a chance to do it again. Studying the tracks outside his cabin had become a habit with Vance, but he was not afraid to go away for a few days, even on a questionable venture such as this one.

Vance came out of his reverie and noted his surroundings. The trail had narrowed, with the land rising up on the right and falling away on the left. Tip and the pack-horse had moved in behind Fred, so Vance rode last. As he looked at the Dunham brothers, he felt disassociated from them. Fred's tendency to see things as through a warped lens, coupled with Tip's tendency to adopt Fred's notions wholesale, gave Vance the feeling once again that this chase was not what it had seemed at the outset: a quest to get even. Maybe it was the whiskey talking, but comments about gelding a man came from somewhere. Vance rather thought that deep down, Fred wanted to geld Rusk but found it easier to transfer the threat to the Mexican. Why he would want to do either, or even think about it, seemed like a twisted response to the death of one's brother. Getting even should call for bringing the others to account, either by hauling them in to the law or by putting a bullet through them.

As the trail wound onward between the ridges on the right and foothills on the left, the atmosphere of the group seemed to get keener. Vance could tell that the other two expected to catch their quarry today, and he himself felt the possibility. The pursuit carried an air of purpose as the riders kept their horses at a brisk pace, varying from a fast walk to a trot, sometimes to a lope to finish an uphill climb, but never back to anything pokey. Then, when the sun was just a bit short of its high point, they began to see tracks again.

"These are new," Fred declared. "They've been put down since yesterday afternoon."

The pursuers kept up their pace. At midday they stopped long enough to water the horses and to eat some jerky that Fred brought out, and then they were on their way again.

Later that afternoon, when the sun had warmed the day and had crossed over to shine in their faces, Fred made an abrupt halt as the trail crested a hill. He held up his hand to bring the others to a stop.

"There's someone up ahead," he said. "It looks like they've got a camp."

He reined his horse around and led the

party back downhill a ways. When he dismounted, the other two did. Handing his reins to Vance, Fred went to his saddlebag on the off side, and after some rooting around he took out a pair of binoculars. Then he bowlegged up the hill, leaning forward and keeping his head down. As he neared the crest he took off his hat, got down on his knees and elbows, and then flattened out to peer through the field glasses.

Vance could feel tension in the air. His heartbeat had picked up, and both he and Tip had their attention focused on Fred, who shifted position a couple of times and then let out a long, low oath.

"What is it?" called Tip.

Fred turned around to a sitting position, put on his hat, and came sidestepping down the hill. "Son of a bitch," he said, shaking his head.

"Is it them?"

"It's not who we thought it was." Fred's hands were trembling as he handed the binoculars to his brother. "You can see for yourself, but I know for sure what I saw this time."

"Rusk and the Mexican?"

Fred shook his head. "There's no Mexican there. It's a man with a beard, all right, which I take to be Rusk, and a woman. Marianne."

Tip let out a heavy breath. "The hell."

"See for yourself. It's just him and her, and two horses. No one else."

"That's a fine mess," said Vance. "Then there never was any Mexican. Rusk would have taken Moon on by himself. If someone was waiting in the shadows and rode off with him, it was her." He could picture Marianne as he knew her, with dark hair to her shoulders. Some Mexican.

"That's the way it seems." Fred dragged his shirt sleeve across his brow. "Go ahead," he said to his brother.

Tip set his hat on his saddle horn and walked up the hill, then settled into place and stayed there for a few minutes. When he came down the hill, he had an uncertain look on his face.

"It's her, all right, but I don't know what we're going to be able to do now."

Fred, who seemed to have regained some of his composure, said, "Let's go back down to a level spot and think it over. They're not goin' anywhere for a while."

Tip gave Fred a knowing look as he handed him the binoculars, and in that moment, Vance understood why the party up ahead had not been traveling fast.

At the bottom of the hill, the men led the horses to water. Fred had dug out his cigarette makings when he put the binoculars away, and now he rolled himself a cigarette. After he lit it, he spoke.

"It wouldn't do to ride down there now, and who knows if they'll even put their clothes on before dark. I imagine they're dug in for the night, so we can just set our camp here and keep an eye on 'em."

"What are you thinkin' on doin'?" asked Tip.

Fred swelled up as he took a drag from his cigarette and blew away the smoke. "We can do whatever in the hell we want. We've got him three to one. Granted, there's a woman there to witness it, but we can shoot him like a buck deer in his bed if we want to. My preference is to go in and call him out when he's on his feet. Do it right in front of her. Make him eat crow, and then if we have to, finish him off."

Vance had to dip his head and swallow before he could talk. "I don't like the idea of goading a man into a fight so you can kill him in front of a woman. If it goes that far, I don't want to be part of it."

Fred spit with the tip of his tongue to clear away a fleck of tobacco. "By God, if we came this far and lost one man already, we've sure as hell got a right to do some-thing."

Vance felt a kick in his stomach. Now that Fred could blame it on someone else, he could acknowledge what happened to Shorty. "Look here," he said. "Let's not go off half-cocked. You ought to think about what you've actually got a right to do. This fellow may have killed your brother, but he didn't have anything to do with Shorty. Keep it straight, Fred."

"By God, I'm keepin' it straight. We've caught up with this son of a bitch, we've got him three to one, and we're in the right." He lifted his arm to take another pull on his cigarette and then said, "I'm goin' to go piss."

Vance wanted to answer, but Fred turned his back on the others and stomped off toward some willows. That was like Fred, to cut off the conversation so he could keep someone from objecting.

Vance turned to Tip, who had his jaws tight. "You two are into this deeper than I am. That's obvious to all of us. But I just want to say, I wonder how far you should push it."

Tip raised his eyebrows to make a direct gaze. "I agree with Fred. We've come all this way to do somethin', by damn."

"Well, all right. But how far do you want to push it?"

Tip wavered. "I don't know. But I know we've got to do something."

Fred came back and rustled in his saddlebag until he pulled out one of the packages he had acquired from Wynn Gregory. He unwrapped the bottle and handed the newspaper to his brother. "Here. You can start a fire with this. I'm goin' to sit down."

While Fred sat on a rock and uncorked the bottle, Vance held the horses. Tip untied Fred's bedroll and tossed it to him, then began to untie the pack on the fourth horse.

"Throw me my duffel bag, too."

Tip did as he was told and went back to untying the lashes. Out of the corner of his eye, Vance could see Fred rummaging around in his bag and then pausing. He would be rubbing his lucky charm.

Vance and Tip unloaded all the gear but left the horses saddled. It was not evening yet, and depending on how things looked in the other camp, they might take a ride over there before nightfall. Fred sat by himself, brooding, as the other two sorted the gear into piles. Then, out of the blue, he said, "That's right. We'll do it right in front of her. Let her see who's a man and who isn't."

Vance took a rope and walked away from camp to string up a picket line. Finding two young cottonwoods the right distance apart, he tied one end and then pulled the rope straight. As he tied off the second end, he wondered about Fred's last comment and put it together with some of his earlier remarks. The realization grew upon him that in some transferred sort of way, Fred wanted to punish Rusk for his intimacy with Marianne and wanted to prove something to her, win her over in some way. Fred was fixed on the whole idea of Marianne giving herself to this other man. Vance felt he had been right in his earlier suspicion that Fred wanted to geld Rusk. Now he thought he had a clearer sense of why. Whether he was aware of it or not, Fred seemed to have the desire that men had when they knew a woman had stepped out, and out of that desire he wanted to do with Marianne what he couldn't do with Charlotte — punish someone. That was getting even for something else, way different from what Fred had stated and Tip had repeated. But it was getting even, and it all blended together.

Vance plucked at the picket line, hesitating before he went for the horses. *A man had a right to get even.* Damned if he hadn't been doing some version of the same thing. For all of Fred's blustering and clamoring, the two of them had more in common than Vance had wanted to admit. But there was a difference. When Vance looked into himself, he didn't want to carry it any further. He didn't feel a need to prove anything, not at this point. He had come this far not to do something, it seemed, but to find out why he had come. Seeing himself in Fred had done it. As far as he was concerned, he was finished with this business, but he knew he was in too deep to ride away from it now. For one thing, he had to look after Tip. For another, he needed to make his break in a way that wouldn't make him look like a quitter.

He thought of the two antelope he had seen on the hillside in the afternoon sun the day before, when he and the others were first riding into the pass. The pair had seem unbothered by the passing horsemen. And now, as Vance stood near the creek and thought of all the greenery and wildlife he had seen along the river and the creek in the last couple of days, a placid world minding its own business, he wondered why men had to push themselves to get even on scores that were so tenuous. Animals had balls, too, and some of them died with their horns locked, but they didn't take it this far.

When he had the horses tied, he decided he wanted to look over the crest of the hill himself, without the binoculars. He just wanted to see the layout for himself, to see what the place looked like and to see that the others were there.

As he peeked over the ridge, he could see the country below in full light, as the sun still hung above the farthest hill. From where he crouched, the trail sloped away into something of a valley, where the pass widened out into low-rolling sage and grassland. Three or four miles in the distance, he could see a gap where it looked as if the last high ridge met the foothills. Beyond the gap, the plains lay in golden sunlight. Bringing his glance back to the scene below, he realized that this was where they would make their play if they were going to do it.

Raising his eyes again for a broad view, he recalled a time a few years back when he had been in the mountains several miles south of here, also looking west at a pass between two sets of mountains. He had remembered the scene many times — the tall, dark trees on the left or south side, the mountain rocky and bare on the right, and a marsh below. He had watched a water bird as it floated across a pond, climbed out, walked a ways, and flew up and up, then circled around and settled in a stand of tall fir trees. It had flown in behind a dead tree. Vance hadn't been close enough to see what kind of a bird it was — just a pale, long-necked bird that was big enough to be visible at dusk, more than half a mile away — but he had heard that herons nested in tall timber, and he thought it might be a heron. It had been a peaceful scene, one he had treasured, and it came back to him now, like the memory of the two antelope relaxed on the hillside, to make him appreciate life without turmoil.

Back at camp, he could see that Fred had not worked very far into the bottle. That was good. He might be a little more reasonable this way.

"See anything?" asked Fred.

"Not much. They're still there. And it's still good daylight."

"Then we might have time to do something."

Vance took a deep breath. "I hope you're not thinking of staging an attack, or riding in there and keeping them at gunpoint."

Now that they had caught up with the other party, Fred had no doubt thought things over as well. "That's two ways," he said, "but there's others."

"I think we should talk with them first."

Fred sniffed. "We can talk, but we'd better settle somethin', one way or the other."

"How do you mean that?"

"I mean, I expect to get some kind of satisfaction from this son of a bitch that killed my brother and took his wife."

"You might cut that in half, Fred. Whatever's she's done with this fella, she's done of her own free will."

"I'll cut him in half, that's what."

Vance could tell that Fred was bothered by the knowledge that Marianne had chosen to leave with Rusk and to do the things she had done, and he guessed that the knowledge had worn away some of Fred's confidence now that he was confronted with it at close range. He still had his resentment and plenty of talk, but he wasn't as swelled up with his own certainty.

Vance went on. "I don't like the idea of forcing a fight right away. I think someone should go talk to them first, not just all three of us show up with guns drawn. You don't know what could go wrong that way." He looked at Tip. "Don't you think so?"

Tip wagged his head back and forth. "I guess, but I agree with Fred that we should get some kind of satisfaction."

"Maybe so, but I'm talking about how to go about it to begin with. If you want to shoot first and then ask questions, I'm out of it. But if you want to go about it with a little more caution, I'm still in. If Fred wants to dress him down in front of her, maybe he'll get a chance." Vance paused and then went on. "Look at it this way. There's just one of him. One of us can go first, and then we take it from there."

Tip looked at Fred, who said, "I think it would be pretty stupid for one of us to go alone. What the hell did we come together for, if we're going to do it that way?"

Vance nodded. "I can see your point about either of you two going alone. There's grudge written all over this thing. But neither of you two has to go. I will."

Chapter Eleven

Tip came down the hill with the binoculars. "They're startin' to build a fire, and they're movin' around normal."

Vance looked at the hillside to the east, still shining in the sun. "There's still plenty of daylight, isn't there?"

"Oh, yeah. Plenty."

"Then I guess I'll go." Vance could feel a nervousness, centered in his stomach and spreading outward, as he went to the picket line and untied his horse. He didn't expect any trouble with Rusk, as he didn't have a personal quarrel with the man. But Rusk did have the capacity for violence, so Vance wasn't going to walk into the scene with his hands in his pockets. Before he put his foot in the stirrup, he checked his six-gun to see that it was loaded and would draw clear. Then he mounted up and rode off.

Up the hill and down he went, not taking any care to be quiet. He rode in the middle of the trail, jogging along. At the bottom of the hill where the road leveled out, the camp lay ahead on the left in the midst of a few scrubby trees that looked like box elders. Two horses were picketed farther back. It was open country here, mostly bare on all sides except for sagebrush and grass.

As Vance turned off the trail toward the camp, a man stepped out into the open. He was an average-sized man with a narrow-brimmed hat and a beard that wasn't very dark. He had his arms at his sides with his right hand not far from the butt of his six-gun and his left holding a coiled rope.

"Hello the camp," Vance called out.

"Come on in."

Vance dismounted and walked the last thirty yards, his reins in his left hand. Slow and easy, he told himself. When he was within ten yards of the other man, he asked, "Are you the fellow named Rusk?"

"That I am." Rusk held a steady gaze as he answered.

Vance stopped about ten feet from the other man. He could see now that Rusk's beard was starting to run to gray, and he had quick green eyes. He had normal features and a medium build, with the hard, solid look of a man who spent time in the saddle. Just by his looks, he was not remarkable in any way.

"My name's Vance Coolidge."

The eyes narrowed. "I don't believe I know you, but apparently you know me — or of me."

"I'm with Fred and Tip Dunham."

"Moon's brothers."

Vance was impressed that Rusk did not hesitate to say Moon's name. "That's right. I came along, or so it seems, to have a level head in the bunch."

"Uh-huh. So where are they?"

Vance motioned with his head. "On the other side of the hill. We've got a camp set there."

Rusk's mouth turned down. "Well, that's handy. I suppose if the bunch of you followed me all this way, it wasn't just to camp next door. What do they want?"

"Well, for most of the way, if you don't mind my saying it, they wanted to have it out with you."

Rusk gave a light shrug. "I can see that."

"But when they found out who you were traveling with, it kind of changed things. It didn't seem like such a good idea to just come stormin' in."

"From what I know of Fred, I wouldn't expect the better judgment to be all his."

Vance felt a ripple of resentment. Even

though Rusk was right, Vance still had a basic loyalty to the Dunham brothers and didn't like such a casual slap. "Well, however it came around, we decided to come and talk first."

"All right." Rusk twisted his mouth and let his gaze relax, then looked at Vance again. "Well, then what comes next? Did you come to tell me something, ask me something? What do they want?"

"I guess the same thing I said before. They want to have it out with you. But rather than shoot first, I think they want to call you on it."

Rusk frowned. "You mean the three of you line up and call me out?"

"No. If that was it, I wouldn't have come down here, and I wouldn't ride in three to one to gun a man down in front of a woman."

"I can appreciate that." Rusk gave a half-smile.

"I think what they want is to call you on it in front of Marianne, and see which way the chips fall."

The eyes narrowed again. "How do you mean?"

"Well, they didn't come right out and say it, but I think they want to see if you can answer to them in front of her."

Rusk held his hands out from his sides, the left hand still holding the rope and the right hand showing its palm. "You mean they want to talk me down, make me look bad or cheap, and see if they can get her to leave me."

"Maybe something like that."

"Aw, hell, I can do that. Do they think they can make her leave me, and then they can come after me? Not that I think it would happen."

"To tell you the truth, I don't know how far ahead they've thought. I just know they want to call you on it."

"Well, that much doesn't scare me. Go ahead and tell 'em we'll be waitin' to talk to 'em whenever they get here."

"Good enough." As Vance turned to lead his horse away, he had the thought that Rusk was on the square. Vance doubted that the man would pull a gun until someone else did, and in spite of the fellow's sarcasm and bluntness, Vance had to admire his nerve. The man had sand.

Back at camp, Fred and Tip were standing up and waiting when Vance rode in.

Fred raised his head in a questioning gesture. "What's he have to say?"

Vance swung down from his horse before

answering. "He says he'll talk to you. The two of you."

"Is she there?"

"Marianne? I guess so. I didn't see her, but I told Rusk you wanted to hash things out in front of her."

"You told him that?"

"Yeah. He asked me what you wanted, and that was more or less how I put it. I said you wanted to call him on it or make him answer to you with her there. I don't know what else I was supposed to say."

"No, I guess that's it."

"I told him I wasn't going to be any part of riding in there, the three of us, and just opening fire on him in front of her."

Fred shook his head. "No, at this point we're just gonna go palaver."

Vance stood with his reins in his hand, waiting for the other two to move. As they went for their horses, he thought about the turn that things had taken when they found out who was with Rusk. On the one hand, the discovery seemed to make Fred eager to lord it over Rusk, like rubbing a dog's nose in its mess. On the other hand, the presence of Marianne, or the knowledge of her presence, seemed to take away some of Fred's cocksureness, as if he were afraid of how he would look to her if things didn't go his way. Vance recalled Fred's banter with Gregory about liking to win, and now he imagined that Fred, who up until now was sure he was going to come out on top, was not worried about his life but about saving face in front of Marianne.

Fred and Tip led their horses to the edge of camp, where they mounted up. Vance swung aboard, and the three of them headed up the hill again. Over the top, Vance saw that the sun still had not slipped below the far ridge, but the shadows were lengthening in the little valley.

As they approached the other camp, Rusk came out and stood as before. A movement farther back caught Vance's eye, and he saw Marianne standing a few steps behind her companion.

Vance rode alongside Fred on the right. "I'll hold the horses," he said.

Fred nodded and made a quarter-turn of his head toward Tip, who gave a quick nod of agreement.

At about twenty yards out, the riders dismounted. Vance took the horses and stayed to the right, while Tip walked a few feet to Fred's left. Five yards from the edge of the camp, they stopped.

Fred's voice had a challenging tone as he

opened the meeting. "Are you Rusk?"

"I am."

"I'm Fred Dunham. Moon's brother."

"Go ahead. Say your piece."

Fred didn't seem prepared to have to speak again without having gotten a real response. After a short silence he said, "I understand you shot my brother."

Rusk's eyes held steady on Fred. "It was a fair fight, one on one. He called me out, told me to meet him on the edge of town. I did, and I managed not to let him get the best of me."

"You killed him."

"No less than he would've done to me."

Fred waited a few seconds as he put on a contemptuous expression. "You came to town lookin' for trouble."

"I'll tell you something I think you already know. Your brother carried trouble with him everywhere he went. If someone had to deal with him, there was going to be trouble of some kind. No one had to look for it with Moon."

Vance noted again that Rusk had no qualms about mentioning names.

"He was my brother."

"That's all good and fine, and you've got a right to be worked up. But to others he was a two-bit crook and a bully. And like I said, it's not as if it was something you didn't know already."

"I'll tell you what I want to know, and that's how you came to have a fight with him."

"I already told you. He was the one that made the challenge."

Fred's face had a hard set to it, overlaid with the dull shine of old sweat. "It's not as if you just happened to be in town." He lifted his head toward Marianne. "You were nosin' around where you had no business."

Vance had the impression that Fred had moved to the next line of argument because he didn't have a way of refuting what Rusk said about Moon. Whatever Fred's motive, he was prepared to take things to a personal level.

The other man was not ruffled. "Let's not let the pot be callin' the kettle black about puttin' your nose in someone else's business," he said. "If you've got a quarrel with me, it's about the fight I had with your brother, not about anything that went on elsewhere."

Fred swelled as he took a breath. "What I'm sayin' is, you came around makin' a play for someone else's wife."

Vance caught a glimpse of Marianne.

She did not wince or look ashamed. She just stood there, very much as Vance remembered last having seen her, except that her dark hair was a little longer. She was calm, and her blue eyes were steady as she watched the two men.

Rusk answered, "Oh, don't get too righteous here. It's no less than Moon did when he got a chance somewhere, and unless I miss my bet, you've tried the same. So we've got the pot-and-kettle problem all over again."

Fred's voice took on a menacing tone that Vance recognized. "I think you've got a lot of damn cheek to come meddlin' around another man's wife and then killin' him for it."

"If it was that simple, maybe I would have a lot of cheek. But it wasn't. If your brother's wife had had enough of him, he did something to help her get that way. But that doesn't concern you, and neither does anything that's gone on between her and me."

Vance could tell Fred's anger was mounting as he said, "I just think you've got a lot of damn gall."

Rusk gave him a sterner look. "And I'm trying to impress on you that you'd do just as well if you didn't have your nose in other people's underwear."

The comment had the effect of a punch that would rock a man back on his heels.

Rusk went on. "Stick to what you really have a quarrel about, and that's the fight I had with Moon. And I'll tell you again, short. He called me out. He got what he asked for. And if you want to start diggin' up personal faults, he had a long list, and several of 'em got him to where he was the other day."

Fred seemed to search for an answer and find none. Then he shifted his gaze to Marianne. "So this is what it comes to, huh? You run off with a man who killed your husband, after everything else."

She was calm as she answered. "It's like Jim said. Moon was trouble. He was a crook and a bully. He brought his end on himself when he tried to force me to come back to him."

"You had no business leaving in the first place."

Marianne gave him a look of tolerance. "It's nothing you would know or have a reason to know. He made me do things against my will in the past, and I had decided I wasn't going to let him do it again."

Vance saw her blue eyes flashing as she

answered straight back at Fred. She had her pride, all right, and she wasn't going to let someone shame her.

Still, Fred's answer was almost a dismissal. "I don't see where anything he could have done was all that bad."

She held her head up as she said, "Maybe you wouldn't."

"Depends on what it was."

She gave a slight shake to her head. "Nothing that's any of your business. Suffice it to say that he thought he had the right. And he didn't, and when he tried it the last time — well, he was warned."

Vance looked at Rusk, then back at Marianne as he developed a better sense of her. She was a woman who had been reached by a man other than her husband, and as such she would attract other men, as might be the case with Fred. But she did not stir anything of that nature in Vance. He saw her simply as a woman who had decided for herself how she was going to do things. She had no air of apology about her, and no brazenness.

After a pause she looked at Fred and Tip both. "I've got nothing against either of you," she said. "But you should just go back. Nothing you can say or do is going to change my course, no more than it can change the things Moon did and what happened to him."

As silence hung in the air for another moment, Vance looked again at Marianne and Rusk. He could understand why she would leave a man like Moon, who more than before was shaping up as something of a crook as well as a bully in areas that Vance declined to imagine. Nor could Vance find anything to hate in Rusk even when he did not approve of what the man had done. Everything washed even with these two, without anything coming out as black and white.

Meanwhile, Fred was still not through, in spite of having been rebuffed by both of the others. Swelling again in the way that he did when he rubbed his lucky charm, he looked down at Marianne and said, "I think you have the money."

The comment, which seemed to Vance to come out of nowhere, seemed to take her by surprise as well.

"What money?" she asked.

"The money he trimmed from a couple of other fellows."

"I don't know exactly what money you're talking about. Moon trimmed money from one place and another, but I don't have any of the proceeds and never did. If Moon ever had any amounts of cash, he piddled it away, and I never saw any of it."

"It was a couple of fellows I don't need to mention by name," Fred answered in a smug tone, as if he might know a little more than the others. "But Winslow and Ludington work for them."

It occurred to Vance that Winslow and Ludington might have had a reason to take care of Moon themselves, but had been content to find out someone else had done it. That was an interesting angle. They really were like buzzards.

Marianne gave a light shrug. "What if they do?"

"Suffice it to say that they're out on the trail here somewhere."

"I don't see why that should worry me."

Fred went on, with his renewed confidence. "I'll tell you this much. I think they're after either your group or ours, whoever they think has the money."

Vance noticed that Fred didn't say he already had a run-in with Winslow and Ludington, and he took Fred's omission as an indication that Fred assumed that the two hardcases didn't think the brothers had the money. It also gave Vance a glimmering of why Winslow and Ludington were out trailing the Dunham party in the rough country south of Medicine Bow and why they might have sent someone like Emerson Prophet to tag along and pick up information from the inside. They were perched, waiting to make a move.

Marianne shook her head again. "If that's the case, they would have done better to have caught up with him sooner, when they had the chance. It's pretty late now."

Vance figured it might have saved quite a few people quite a bit of trouble if Winslow and Ludington had done things that way, but now everyone was stuck with the way things had happened.

"Maybe it is," Fred answered. "But they don't necessarily know that. They think someone still has the money, and they're looking for satisfaction." He looked at Rusk. "And I can't blame them for thinkin' that the money might have been one of the reasons you did what you did."

Vance was stunned with the cheekiness of Fred's comment, but Rusk didn't let it get under his skin.

"If they were to think that," he said.

Fred shrugged as if he had a much better position than the other two. "I couldn't say for sure, but whether you've got the money or not, you might want to remember that there's two of them, and they're not always that particular about how they do things."

"Maybe that explains why they were in cahoots with Moon. Birds of a feather. But they can't get something from us if we don't have it."

"Suit yourself," Fred snipped.

"You do the same. And now that we've been through the topic of some money that Moon swindled, is there anything else?"

Fred seemed to come up empty again, as if he hadn't expected the parley to end so soon. "I think so far I've said what I came to say, and that's the reasons I've got no use for you."

"Well, then, I guess we're done." Rusk looked at Tip. "Unless you've got something to say."

Tip, who had not said a word during the whole meeting, shook his head in the negative.

Fred came back in his contentious tone. "No, we're not done," he said. "Not by a long ways."

Vance wondered what Fred meant by "we" — whether it meant Fred and Tip, their party of three, or the Dunhams and Rusk together. Maybe Fred didn't know for sure, either, but just wanted to make sure he got in a contradictory remark.

Whatever the case, Rusk didn't answer. He just nodded and let the visitors be on their way. As Tip and Vance began to straighten out their reins, Fred lingered.

"This is a mighty poor way to do things, Marianne," he said.

"It's been poor all along. All of it."

"Well, like I said, we're not done."

Vance turned and saw her blue eyes, still steady and bright as she answered Fred one more time.

"You should be."

Fred lifted his head in defiance, then turned and mounted his horse. Tip and Vance swung into the saddle as well, and the three of them trotted away from the camp.

As he rode in the silent company of the two brothers, Vance had clear images of Rusk and Marianne, both of them cool and unbothered by Fred and his impertinent manner. Thinking back on the whole encounter, Vance found himself neither admiring nor despising Rusk but just accepting the way things had gone. He might have felt as neutral about Marianne if there hadn't been something in her bearing that gained a measure of his sympathy. Men could call her what they wanted, but she chose her own way and did not back down. It occurred to Vance that the shine in her blue eyes did not come only from defying Fred. Somewhere in the mess, though no one had said anything about it, she must have had some genuine feelings for Rusk that did not proceed from her troubles with Moon. Rusk had been confident in her, and the two of them had stood like partners in answering their visitors. Then it occurred to him that they might be the man and wife to whom Joe Nanno had referred.

Still picturing Marianne's blue eyes, Vance felt something there that touched him, and it wasn't in a way that aroused his desire. Quite the opposite, he realized now: it reminded him of Josie. Whatever Josie had had with Nate Cousins, it had meant something to her and didn't have much to do with Vance. He realized it must not have been easy for her, and he did not have to take it as something personal that happened to him.

It seemed like a small lesson to learn after having come all this way and having lost a good friend, but at least it was something. As Vance looked at the two brothers, he doubted that Fred had learned even that much. And as for Tip, that remained to be seen.

Chapter Twelve

Tip said nothing all the way back to camp, and even when he handed his horse to Vance to put it out to graze, he just shook his head. Vance wasn't sure how to take it — anger, disgust, renunciation, or dissatisfaction — so he said nothing in return as he took the three horses and led them away.

He set the horses out at fair distances from one another, each on its own picket. In the fading light of evening he could see where the grass grew the best and where there were no stumps for the horses to wind their ropes around. When he had the three saddle horses staked out, he fetched the packhorse from the picket line and set it out as well. The cut on its front foot seemed about the same, but at least it wasn't getting any worse. Vance assumed he and the Dunhams would all head back home in the morning, and if they didn't have the kinds of delays they had on the way out, they might be able to make it in two days.

That was the reasonable view of things.

But for all he knew, dealing with Fred might have more turns to it. As Vance went to gathering firewood, he recalled the words — *we're not done* — and wondered how much of Fred's declaration was a threat he meant to make good on and how much was a bluff. He had said it twice, so maybe he had his mind set on another confrontation. If he did intend to go back for more, he would probably take another tack, as he had not fared well in open debate. Even now, he was probably stewing over the way he had been talked down to and cut off at every turn. If he were going to give it another try, he was going to have to marshal his forces in a different way. Vance hoped he did nothing of the sort, but as Shorty had said, Fred had some kinks in his rope. The more Vance thought about it, the more he imagined it was all too probable that Fred wouldn't know when to quit.

Vance got his first indication when he returned to camp with an armload of firewood. Fred was sitting on his bedroll with the bottle on the ground between his feet. Tip, with his hat next to him, was sitting on his own bedroll at a right angle to Fred, and no one had lifted a finger to get the evening meal going.

Fred was talking, and from the blunted edges in his voice, Vance imagined the whiskey was making itself felt.

"That's what I should have done, by God. Less talk and more action. I should have just walked up to him, grabbed him by the front of his shirt, and asked him who in the hell he thought he was. But like a dummy, I went there to talk. That's their game, not mine. And what did Pa always say, huh? Don't play the other man's game. And I fell right into it."

"You got to take the lead," said Tip. "That's what we didn't do. All the time we were standing there, that was what was going wrong." He leaned forward and held out his hand.

Fred picked up the bottle by its neck and, leaning forward himself, tilted the bottom toward Tip. "Make 'em play our game, that's what. That'd set Marianne back to doin' what she ought to be doin', and that's standin' back with her mouth shut and watchin'." Fred raised his doubled fist in the gloom. "And as for Rusk, I'd like to give him one of these, and then another. That's what."

Tip pulled the cork out of the bottle with a squeak. "I'm not good at talkin'," he said, then took a sip of whiskey and lowered the bottle. "But if it comes to throwin' a few punches, I can hold my own."

Fred held his hand out for the bottle, and as he took it back into his possession, he said, "He talks a good fight, that's what. And he says this 'n' that. He says he beat Moon in a fair fight, but who's to say? Whoever saw it sure as hell didn't see much if they thought there was a Mexican in on it. The way I heard it, the two of them jumped Moon. I kind of doubt that, now. That is, I doubt that these two jumped him. But there's room to doubt that it was a fair fight. But with two of us and only one of him, we could make sure it stayed fair." Fred tipped himself a drink.

Vance took the opportunity to get in a word. "Is anyone goin' to build a fire, or shall I do it?"

Fred gave him a backward wave of the hand. "We'll get to it. No one's in a hurry." He poked the cork into the neck of the bottle and hit it with the heel of his right hand. "We're talkin' about how we ought to handle that son of a bitch."

"I can tell."

Fred raised his eyes in a sullen glare. "You can tell. I suppose you can tell a lot, but I can tell you something. This son of a bitch didn't kill a brother of yours. But he did ours. And we're not done with him."

"That's up to you. What I was concerned with was whether we were goin' to get a fire started."

"Go ahead. Burn all the wood in this canyon for all I care."

"I'll do it," said Tip. "Go ahead and sit down, Vance."

"No, I'll go get some more firewood while there's still a little light. Then I'll slice off some steaks when I get back."

"Fine. I'll start the fire in a couple of minutes."

Vance walked back out into the dusky evening to look for more wood. He could tell that the meeting at the other camp had left both of the brothers unsettled, and now they were rebuilding their defiance. It was going to be a long evening, he thought, if he had to put up with the two of them nipping on the bottle.

When Vance got back to camp, Tip had a fire going and was seated on his bedroll as before, but with his hat on. Vance laid his second armload of firewood on top of the first.

"That's a pretty good heap of wood," Tip said.

"If tonight's anything like last night, we'll be glad we've got it."

"White man build big fire, stand way back," said Fred in an apparent attempt to be humorous. When no one responded, he spoke again. "That's what an Indian told me one time. 'Indian build little fire, stay real close. White man build big fire, stand way back.' "

Vance decided to go along if Fred was trying to be good-natured. "I guess they do. I knew a fellow who said he got separated from his friends up in the mountains one time. They were huntin' elk, and it was later in the year, when it gets dark early. Said he had to spend the night out in the woods on his own. Temperature got down to about forty below, and he built a hell of a big fire and still almost froze to death."

"Lots of ways to die," Fred remarked. "That's one of 'em, and it'd make you wish you'd paid more attention." Then, as if he was satisfied with his own idea, he said, "That's right. And not enough people think about it."

"Uh-huh." So much for the good humor, Vance thought. Fred was bound to circle back to the same topic, no matter what. Then out loud he said, "I'll go ahead and cut those steaks now."

Tip had mixed up a batter of quickbread in one skillet and had set it at the edge of the fire, and now the first bubbles were forming in what promised to be something like a huge, heavy pancake. As Vance got out the deer meat and cut off the steaks, he caught an occasional glance at Tip. Squatting on his heels, Tip did not wobble, but he seemed a bit slow and dull as he fried the first couple of slices of bacon and greased the skillet for the steaks. When Vance handed him the deer meat, he said, "Thanks," in a voice that sounded subdued.

Fred spoke up again. "Yep. Lots of ways to die. And you never know how it's goin' to happen to you. You take this fellow Rusk, for example. He probably wasn't worried about dyin' this afternoon. But you know, it could have happened. We could have just rode in there, told him this was what you get, and done it."

Vance took an impatient breath. "The reason we rode in the way we did was that we weren't goin' to shoot first. If you ride into someone's camp with no warning at all, there's no tellin' whether you'll get a belly of lead yourself."

"Not from that son of a bitch. But no matter. We decided to do things one way, and we did. If we'd done 'em in another, we might have taken care of him and be finished by now. But we aren't."

Vance held his tongue. If Fred wanted to talk about all the things he wished he had said and done, then he could just go ahead and talk all night long. Meanwhile, there would be steak and a fire.

Fred reached for the bottle. "But like we said, it would've been hard to do with her there. She could watch him shoot Moon and never peep a word, but let someone put a bullet in Shit-face, and you don't know what kind of witness she might bear against you." He squeaked out the cork again and then paused with the bottle wavering at chest height. "That's the way it went today, but the next time we'll do things our way, not play their game."

Vance felt a little twitch of alarm. "What do you think you're going to do?" he asked.

Fire leaped into Fred's eyes as he held the bottle closer and licked his lips. "Hammer the son of a bitch, that's what! We're not gonna let him get away with it."

Vance looked at Tip, who seemed to be straining to keep his eyelids raised as he leaned toward the fire. Then, turning back to Fred, Vance said, "Hammer him. Do you mean the two of you are going to try to thrash him?"

"One of us will, and the other one can stand by to keep things clean. By God, we'll pound him into the ground." Fred took a drink.

"What do you mean, keep it clean, if you're going against him two to one?"

Fred winced as the whiskey went down. "If he goes for a gun, we go for one."

"So you want to goad him into the kind of a fight where you've got a chance to shoot him, after all?"

"He's going to pay one way or the other." The dull face wavered, as if its owner were floating. "The son of a bitch thinks he's smart. Takes a man's woman, kills the man for complainin', then smirks at the man's brothers, with the woman standin' by just admirin' the whole thing. Well, I'll tell you, he's been dancin' and now he's gonna pay the fiddler."

Vance took a deep breath. He wondered how much of the renewed rant was bluster, brought on by the whiskey at a safe distance from the separate intimidations of Rusk and Marianne. "What if things don't go your way?" he asked.

Fred's face tightened. "Things will. This ain't my first night away from the farm."

Vance took a few more measured breaths. He realized he had let himself get drawn into an argument, so he decided to try to hold his tongue again.

The smugness returned and the face wavered. "Look here. I'll tell you how things go."

Vance raised his chin to see how the steaks were cooking.

"I said, look here, Vance."

Realizing that Fred meant for him to look at something, Vance turned to see Fred with his left hand held out in the firelight. There on his fingers lay the lucky charm.

"Do you know what this is?"

"I have no idea. I just know it's something you carry around. Tip said it was your lucky charm."

"Well, it is."

Vance nodded but refrained from speaking.

"It's something I got."

A shrug and a small nod did not slow down Fred's determination to be heard.

"It's something I got when things went the way they were supposed to."

"Well, fine. Good for you."

"Maybe you'd like me to be more specific."

"It sounds as if you want to be, so go ahead."

Fred swelled up as he held the neck of the bottle in his right hand and stretched his left hand out farther. "This here is a nigger's ear, Vance. A nigger that me 'n' a couple of other fellas strung up because we didn't like the way he acted around a white woman."

Vance felt a wave of disgust flood through him, and he made himself not look at the object in Fred's hand. "That's a fine thing to be proud of," he said. He remembered Fred's earlier boast about wanting to geld the Mexican, and he realized the ear was as good as a pizzle to Fred.

"Actually, it is," Fred answered. "It's a good reminder of how you can make things go your way."

Vance shook his head. "If you think you're going to get me to stand by and help you get the edge on someone for whatever purposes you've got in mind, you're wrong. None of this is worth it. If you had any brains, you'd call it quits and pull out of here first thing in the morning. That's what I'm going to do."

" 'Cause you've got brains. Uh-huh."

Vance made himself not answer.

"Well, I'll tell you. Maybe Tip and I have got no brains, but we've got guts. It was our brother that got killed, and we're gonna even the score one way or the other. If you want to pull out, that's fine. We can take care of it ourselves."

Fred brought out his tobacco and papers and began to build a cigarette. Vance noticed that his movements were slower than usual but not yet clumsy.

Tip jabbed his knife into a deer steak and scooted it in the pan to keep it from sticking. After he moved the other two steaks, he turned his gaze toward Vance.

"I know you don't like the sound of it," he said, "but we can't come all this way and catch him, and not do any more than we've done." He shook his head. "Not after what he did to Moon. All the time I was standin' there, I felt like I had my hands tied and couldn't change the way things were goin'. And we can't just leave it at that. We've got to do more than we did."

Tip, who as a rule didn't talk very much, seemed loosened by the whiskey although his tongue hadn't thickened yet. It was hard to tell how much he had drunk, as Vance had never seen him have more than a drink or two and didn't know what his capacity was.

"Well, I've already said where I stand on

it," Vance said. "If the two of you want to go back for another round, go ahead. I doubt that you need me anyway."

Fred lit his cigarette with a branch he had poked into the edge of the fire. As he tilted his head upward and blew out a plume of smoke, he had the poise of having regained his authority. "No, we don't," he said. "You can wait here with the pack-horse, or you can pull out like you said. Me 'n' Tip can take care of things just fine."

Vance felt as if he were being dismissed, and he realized that Fred wouldn't be so free about it if he didn't have Rusk out-numbered two to one anyway. When Fred thought he had two men to go up against, he wanted four on his side. But now that he knew he had only one opponent, he could be brave and do it with two. That was Fred. He had the courage of a man who needed to have an advantage guaran-teed, like a coward in a mob, and then he could imply that anyone who didn't want to go along was the one who didn't have guts.

Tip spoke as he turned the steaks with his knife. "I'd just as soon you didn't go away sore," he said, "and it's safer to travel in company anyway. But if you don't want to be around to know how things turn out, that's all right."

"We'll see." In the back of his mind, Vance was turning over something incidental that Tip said. It was safer not to travel alone. A fellow like Joe Nanno might be able to breeze through anyone's company, but Winslow and Ludington were out there somewhere, and they hadn't grown any fonder of the Dunham brothers and their friends.

Something of a truce settled in as Fred smoked his cigarette, Vance kept to himself, and Tip continued tending to supper. Vance noticed that the whiskey bottle, which stood on the ground between Fred's feet, had gone down to about a quarter full. As Vance had it figured, there was still another full bottle in Fred's gear. If the two brothers called it good when they got to the bottom of this one, they might be fit to manage a showdown with Rusk in the morning. Otherwise, provided they didn't sleep in too late and let him get away, they would stand a chance of getting hurt.

Fred must have noticed him glancing at the bottle, for he picked it up by the tip of the neck and extended it toward Vance, who shook his head. He felt as if Fred was acting generous as he invited Vance to join the victorious party. At any other time like this, such as at the end of a gather or drive, he would be inclined to take a pull when the bottle was going all the way around; but now, he wasn't going to move an inch in the direction of something he thought was absurd at best.

Vance stared at the coals. This was a strange situation, to have come all this way and to have lost Shorty in the meanwhile, for no good reason, and then to feel stuck with these other two as they worked themselves into a fancied state of valor and virtue. Fred's momentary goodwill did not sway Vance from his conviction that this whole business was wrongheaded. He had become used to Fred's manner, but to see Tip being drawn in to this degree made him feel like an outsider or stranger. Well enough, he thought. At the very least he would stay sober, and in the morning he would decide whether to pull out right away or wait a while.

The steaks came off the fire in good shape, and the quickbread was edible in spite of being crumbly on the outside and soggy in the middle. No one said much as the three of them put away the food. When the plates were stacked, Vance went to the creek for water, and when he got back,

Fred had rolled himself a cigarette and was puffed up into another spell of oratory.

"That's it," he said. "That's the whole thing. We make them play our game from the start, and then they'll see what's what."

Tip nodded and made a swallowing motion as he handed back the bottle. Vance could see that the level had gone down.

"You've gotta ask yourself," Fred went on, "what kind of a man would do the kinds of things he's done, and then you've got to decide what kind of man you are yourself." He took a pull on the bottle. "Me, I'm not the kind to give up just because someone else told me to. I'll tell you, it wouldn't hurt if someone gave her a good slappin'."

Vance held his tongue as he sat down. From what Marianne had said, she had been slapped around, or worse, already, and some of that manly treatment may have helped all of them get to where they were this evening.

Fred set the uncorked bottle between his feet. "It's that thing they've got between their legs that makes 'em think they can do what they want. But if someone makes 'em understand it's not theirs to give or take away as they please, why, they sing a different tune. And they're not so cheeky."

Vance looked at Tip, who again seemed to be working to keep his eyes open. He might be listening, but he wasn't nodding.

Fred, whose dulled features were relaxed at the moment and not tensed in anger, seemed to note that Tip didn't care for the ungallant talk about women. "Gittin' back to Dog-face," he said, "you just got to make sure you make him face up to you." He gave an earnest look toward his younger brother. "You can't let 'em walk all over you. Even if it was somethin' less. But when they've done wrong to your family, to your own flesh and blood, you've got to stand up and be a man."

Tip raised his chin. "Anyone who thinks otherwise about me is in for a surprise."

Fred moved his head in a slow dip of agreement and handed the bottle back to Tip.

Vance stood up. "I'm going to go check the horses," he said, and he walked away into the night. It was hard enough to sit through Fred's talk, but he couldn't stand to watch Tip get drunk and take on the same poses.

He went out and looked at the horses, and seeing nothing out of order, he went back to camp. Neither Fred nor Tip was speaking at the moment, but an air of self-satisfaction prevailed between them. Vance decided he did not want to sit up just to see if they were going to open the second bottle, so he announced his intention to go to bed. As he rolled out his blankets and crawled in, he heard the mutter of Fred's voice, low and indistinct but in its usual authoritative tone.

Vance woke up, not knowing how much time had passed but realizing it had been a while since he had heard the buzz of voices. The camp was silent, and only a faint glow emanated from the campfire. Then came a snoring sound from the direction that would be Fred's. Vance wondered how Tip was doing, and as he peered in that direction, he could make out the form of Tip's bedding still rolled up. He let out a long breath as he gave it a thought. As much as he didn't like getting up out of his own warm bed, he knew he should look after Tip. If the young man was passed out on the ground with a good dose of liquor in his veins, he could get a bad chill.

Vance rolled out of his blankets, leaving them in place to hold what warmth they might. After pulling on his boots, he stood up and moved across the campsite, trying to find the form of a sleeping person some-where on the ground. As he looked, he found a bottle near the fire, and holding it up to the glow of the embers, he saw that it was half full. So the two brothers had worked their way well into the second bottle, and now Tip had wandered off somewhere — most likely to use the bushes — and might have fallen asleep.

Turning to set the bottle back on the ground, Vance saw something that stopped him. A pair of spurs lay on top of Tip's bedroll. Vance didn't like the looks of that. Wherever Tip had gone, he had decided to make as little noise as possible even if he was stumbling drunk.

Vance set down the bottle and squatted next to the fire pit. He could hear Fred snoring, and he felt himself despising the older Dunham. Talk brave, get drunk, pass out, and let the younger brother wander off who knows where. Vance felt a chill. He felt he had too good of a hunch as to where Tip had gone, but until he had better cause, he wasn't going to go meandering off in the dark himself to find out.

Vance woke up, knowing what he had heard. It was a shot, lone and clear and distant in the night. He remembered going back to bed and lying there, wondering, for half an hour or so, and now the sound pulled him from the slumber he had drifted into. He listened for another shot, but it did not come. When a fellow heard a second shot, he could place the first one better, but even without the second one, Vance knew where the first one would have come from.

He put on his hat, pulled on his boots, and went out to gather his horse. Whatever had happened, he needed to get to the other side of the hill and look after Tip.

Saddling the horse by starlight, he put on the bridle and led the animal out to the trail. Then he swung aboard and kicked the horse into a fast walk. As he crested the hill, he could not see very far ahead at all, so he kept the horse to a walk as they moved downhill.

Once the trail leveled out, he listened as closely as he could. Up ahead he could see the faintest flicker of firelight, but nothing shone bright enough for him to see shapes. He wondered if he should call out, and he decided to wait. The small fire told him someone was probably up at the Rusk camp, and if he listened he might get some indication of whether Tip was at the camp or out wandering in the dark.

Then he heard a low moan. He stopped the horse and listened until he heard it again. It was ahead and on the left. Moving forward and stopping again, he placed it closer. He dismounted and led the horse until he found Tip lying on his side and half-propped up on one elbow.

Vance spoke in a low voice. "Tip. It's me, Vance. What the hell happened? Are you all right?"

"Yeah, I'm all right," came the voice, though it sounded slurred and weak.

"What happened?"

"I got shot."

"You damn fool. Where'd he get you?"

"Right here."

"Where's that? I can't see."

Tip's voice had a gasping sound as he said, "Right here, in the ribs."

"You're a damn fool, Tip. What the hell were you doing over here?"

"I came to get the son of a bitch."

"Well, all you got was shot."

"I know."

Vance made himself take a deep breath and exhale. Then he shook his head and said, "Well, there's no point in arguing about it now. Let's get you onto my horse and we'll go back to camp."

"Fred's going to be mad."

"Oh, to hell with Fred. Let's get you onto this horse." This was a hell of a mess, Vance thought as he gave Tip a hand and helped him to his feet. Then, as Tip wobbled, Vance caught him around the waist and felt his shirt, wet and sticky. "Hang on," he said. "We'll get you up onto it, and then we'll get you back to camp."

"Sure," said Tip, steadying himself.

Vance paused, waiting for the moment when it felt as if Tip was ready. "What the hell did you do, just stumble into their camp?"

Tip coughed. "I don't remember for sure. It was all dark. He hollered, and I hollered, I think. Then I was here on the ground, with this pain burnin' through me."

"Did you draw your gun?"

"I don't know. I don't remember."

"Well, it's gone. You don't have it."

"We'd better get it."

"We'll find it later. Right now, we need to get you back to camp."

Vance pushed and boosted Tip into the saddle, then told him to hang on tight. Leading the horse by the reins, Vance walked up and over the hill and took them back into camp. After helping Tip down from the saddle and getting him laid out and covered up, he built up the fire. Then he rousted Fred, who was sleeping the sleep of the very drunk.

Fred sat by Tip with a canteen of water as Vance went out to find more firewood. Once he was by himself, Vance let his anger flow — at Tip for getting drunk and thinking he was going to prove something, and at Fred for working his younger brother up to such a thing. All of this trouble was unnecessary, pointless, starting with Shorty's death and now this.

When Vance came back with an armload, Fred seemed to have come out of his fog enough to have an expression of anguish on his face.

"How's he doing?" Vance asked.

"About the same."

Vance knelt on the other side of Tip's bed. He was angry at Fred well beyond anything he could think or say, but he made himself stay focused on Tip. "You've got to pull through here," he said.

"I know."

"You've got better things to do." Vance could picture Ruth as he had seen her last: a worried young woman on the sidewalk in Rock River.

"That's right."

"You've got to hang on, and we'll get

you back home where you can heal up."

"Uh-huh."

"You've got plenty to live for, Tip." Vance could picture her again, sad-faced, a girl with hair the color of dark straw.

"Oh, yeah."

Fred's voice came up. "He'll be fine. I'll see to it. I'll sit up with him and feed him water. When someone loses a little blood, he gets thirsty."

Vance looked at Tip's face, pale in the firelight. "We could try to patch him up on the outside, but I don't know what to do about where he's bleeding on the inside."

Fred shook his head. "He's not that bad. Go ahead and put the horse away, and we'll both sit up with him if you want."

Vance left the horse saddled and tied him to the picket line. He had it ingrained to keep up a night horse when there might be trouble, so he did, even though he had no idea of what other trouble might come or where he would go for help.

Back at the campfire, he drew his bedding alongside Tip's, as Fred had done. He kept to himself and let the brothers be together, although Tip did not speak. Fred was making small talk about what they were going to do when they got back. After a while he quit talking, and Vance looked across at him. His blond hair and dull face looked gray in the firelight, and Vance could tell from the silence of the moment that Tip was dead.

Chapter Thirteen

Vance was coiling up the picket line when Fred came walking over and told him he wanted to go after Rusk again. Furthermore, he wanted Vance to go with him.

Vance gave a look of disbelief. "You expect me to go?"

"Yes, I do. And I think you can see why."

"I already told you last night I was done with this whole business and wasn't going to help you gang up on anyone."

"That was when there was two of us, me and Tip. Now I'm down to one, and I need you to back me up."

Vance shook his head. "No. I've had enough."

"Things have changed." Fred drew his shoulders back. "I know you didn't care about Moon, but Tip was your friend."

"Of course he was. But that in itself doesn't give me cause."

Fred spit off to the side. "We've got more justification than a man should need, and a damn sight more now than before."

"There wasn't that much to begin with."

Fred's face clouded in anger. "Look here. I've had two brothers die because of that son of a bitch, and I can't let him get away with it."

Vance took a measured breath and tried to pick his words with care. "I've got to reserve judgment on Moon as far as this part about justification goes. That's all between other people. As for Tip, there's no changing what happened. I think he died for a bad cause and his death could have been avoided."

"You'd feel different if it was your brother."

Vance looked at the coil of rope in his hand and then at Fred. "Maybe I would, but it's not as if I don't feel anything at all. He was my friend, and a good one. But his dying doesn't make the original cause any more justified."

Fred seemed to let the last comment sink in. "In other words, you think I took us all on a bad mission."

"That's one way of putting it. And you've acted as if no one has the right to disagree with you on any part of it."

"So you're saying it's all my fault. You're saying it's my fault that Tip got killed."

"No, I'm not. I'm just trying to see things straight if I can. Tip was my friend.

So was Shorty. When I talked to Tip about what happened to Shorty, he said what you said. Shorty should have been more careful."

"He should have."

"Well, I'm saying something similar might apply now."

"So you're saying it was Tip's own fault."

Vance drew his brows together. "I'm saying that if he'd been more careful he'd be alive. I don't know how drunk he was, but I know he had plenty of liquor in him. I imagine it helped him get the idea that he could do something brave. It was deliberate. He thought about it, even if it was in some drunk way. He took off his spurs and left them here. And then he went and barged into someone else's camp in the middle of the night."

"You don't know that's how it happened."

"I know he went there, not the other way around. If he didn't go all the way into Rusk's camp, he was prowling around close enough to get in trouble."

Fred shook his head. "You just don't care."

"I do care. I care that two of my friends have gotten killed. But I don't see enough justification to go after Rusk."

"I do."

"Then go yourself."

Time seemed to stop. Fred's face went hard as a rock. Then after as much as a minute of silence, he said in a tone of bitterness, "You won't go with me for Tip's sake."

Vance shook his head as before. "No. I'm not going to follow one bad action with another."

Fred's anger came out again. "You just don't care about anyone. You're just lookin' after yourself."

"If that was all I was doing, I would have stayed home. I came along because I thought things were one way. They turned out to be another. And even by then I began to have my doubts as to what my own reasons were."

"Well, what were they, then?"

"I guess it came down to the idea that a man had a right to get even."

"Well, by God, none of that has changed."

"I can't say that. There's got to be a damned good reason to begin with. I thought there was, but that changed."

"Nothin' changed. He shit in Moon's bed and then killed him. That's plenty of reason. And then he killed Tip. That's plenty more."

"He shot Tip. He didn't go after him to kill him, or I imagine he would have."

Fred shook his head again and made an expression of contempt. "You just don't care."

"If that's the only way you can put it, then go ahead. But you're not going to push me into picking a fight with someone when I don't believe there's enough cause."

"All you care about is yourself. You don't care about family — not about someone else's, anyway."

Vance had a fleeting picture of Josie and the baby. He did not answer Fred, but he did not look away.

Fred must have taken the response for an opening, for he went on. "You don't care about people's family, their marriages, nothin'."

"I don't think it's fair to say that."

"No, you don't, but it's true. You don't care about someone else's family ties, their brothers —"

"Just a minute. Caring is one thing, and so is respect. I can respect someone else's marriage even if I don't know what goes on in it. And I can care about someone who lost a brother. That's why I came along to begin with. For Tip."

"But you wouldn't do a damn thing for me. I know that."

"Let me finish. I can care about someone else without going off and starting a fight I don't believe in."

Fred shook his head. "You don't care. You just talk. You're like the others." He motioned with his head toward the west.

Vance could feel his own anger building. Fred was as much as saying that if Vance wasn't with him, he was against him. Still trying to stay calm, he said, "If I didn't care, I wouldn't have come along."

"For all I know, you just wanted to get away from your wife for a few days. And I've got nothin' to say on that."

"Well, leave it out, then. And I'm just about done talkin' about any of the rest of it."

"Heartless."

"What?"

"I said you're heartless. Here's my brother, your friend, dead from a bullet hole, and you don't care enough to do something about it."

"If I didn't care, I wouldn't have gone out lookin' for him last night, and he would have died alone in the dark."

"I mean doin' something about it now."

"I told you I'm not going to." Vance turned to walk away.

"I don't think you've got the guts."

Fred's words stopped him, and he turned back. Looking Fred squarely in the eye, he said, "Maybe I don't have what it takes to string up a man and cut off his ear, and maybe I won't help you go get the drop on Rusk, but don't think I've got no guts at all."

"I'm just goin' on what I've seen."

"Well, if you're so brave yourself, just go over there on your own, like I said earlier."

Fred was quiet for another long moment until he said, "All I know is what I've seen."

"What do you mean by that?"

"I haven't seen you lift a finger to stick up for anyone, includin' yourself."

Vance felt his face go tense as his gaze narrowed. "And how is that?"

Fred lifted his head and took on his nonchalant air. "If you want to let someone walk all over you, that's your business. No one'll blame you for raisin' someone else's kid, but they might wonder why you didn't have the guts to do something about it when you could."

Vance swung the coiled rope around and

slapped Fred on the side of the head, knocking his hat askew and raising color where the rope stung his cheek.

Fred's eyes opened and he said, "Why, you coward!"

Vance dropped the rope with his right hand and brought a punch across with his left. Fred went back half a step, knocked his falling hat away, and brought up his fists.

Vance tossed his hat aside and brought up his own fists. "You asked for it, Fred."

Breathing through his nose and keeping his jaw clenched, Fred said nothing as he moved forward. He delivered three quick blows to try to knock down Vance's guard, and when he couldn't get that done, he tried to come around with a right hook.

Vance jerked his head back as the fist sliced the air in front of his nose and chin. Then, moving his weight back onto his toes, he circled to the left, looking for an opening.

Fred came at him again, mauling with both arms and glancing a blow off Vance's left cheek. Vance dropped his left shoulder and came in straight with a right punch. It caught Fred full in the mouth, and Vance could feel both flesh and teeth as he connected. It was a good punch, but it cost him. Before he could move away, Fred pounded a blow on his right temple.

As they both backed off, Vance could see red in Fred's lips. He wondered if Fred was ready to call it quits, but then he found out. Fred came at him again, flailing his fists in roundhouse swings. Vance felt knuckles graze off the top of the left side of his head, and then a blow to the other side set his right ear to ringing. He hunched behind his guard and thrust his left fist through to connect with Fred's right cheek. It stopped Fred short and gave Vance the opportunity to move away.

Fred came at him again, trying to connect more blows to the head. Vance moved back and away, now to one side and now to another. Then he stopped and braced himself as Fred, still moving forward, glanced a fist off the back of his head. Fighting inside, Vance smashed his left fist into Fred's mouth, then drew back his fist and double-punched him in the same place. Next he tried to come around with his right, but he was in too close and it bounced off Fred's shoulder. The two fighters drew apart again.

Fred's breathing was heavy now, and he had his mouth open. Vance could smell last night's whiskey and he could see blood in the crevices between Fred's yellow teeth. He realized his own mouth was open, and he made himself shut it. With his jaw set, he launched forward. Going straight at Fred, he couldn't get past his guard because Fred was taller, but a good try with his left got Fred to bring his guard up high enough that Vance was able to drop his right fist and drive it into Fred's midsection.

Fred grunted, sagging for an instant and then pulling himself together. He had his mouth closed again, and the breaths through his nose sounded heavy.

Vance could feel a burning in the pit of his stomach and his own breath heaved as he tried to keep his gaze steady. One more try, he thought, circling to his left and then bouncing back with a left jab and a right cross. Fred just fended him off and moved back, then turned and vomited.

Vance figured he had done it with the punch to the gut. He stepped back and winced, trying not to see the stream of puke and trying not to smell the rotten whiskey. When Fred came back around with his fists up, his eyes were red and watery.

"I've had enough if you have," Vance said.

Fred wiped his sleeve across his mouth, then turned his forearm and wiped his nose. "I guess so," he said. He dropped his guard and walked back to the campsite, where all this time the body of his brother had lain covered with a blanket.

Vance picked up both hats and his rope and followed Fred to the camp. Handing him his hat, he said, "I'll help you load up everything if you want."

Fred looked around. "I don't care about any of it, but I need to bring Tip back. I couldn't just bury him here."

"Do you want me to ride with you?"

Fred gave his head a slow turn to look at Vance. "I wouldn't ask you for a damn thing at this point. If you won't side with me against the son of a bitch that caused it all, I don't need you to ride back with me when there's nothin' left to do."

Vance shrugged. "I'll go back on my own, then, like I said yesterday. I'll help you get everything loaded, and I'll let you go ahead." He thought the least he could do was ride a ways behind in case Fred needed help with something.

Fred gave him a sullen look. "I don't need anyone to watch my back."

"It's all the same, but I'll wait."

The morning sun was clearing the ridge

in the east when Fred rode away. Vance watched the three horses, each with its own burden, as they disappeared around a bend in the trail. As much as Fred had berated him for not caring, he felt sorry for him. The man had lost two brothers, had one on his conscience whether he wanted to admit it or not, and had a belly full of spite that he had not been able to work out.

Vance went to the creek and knelt by the soothing water. He washed his face and bathed his temples, feeling the spots where he was going to be sore from Fred's punches. It reminded him of the sore spots from the hailstones just a few days earlier. This whole trip had turned into much more of a disaster than he could have imagined, all because getting even seemed like a plausible idea.

He got up and put on his hat. He figured he had a couple of hours to kill if he was going to let Fred have a good head start. He didn't feel like eating or sleeping, even though he had done neither since he had gotten up in the night to go look for Tip. His eyes felt tired, his head buzzed, and he felt as if he were moving in a bubble. He needed to clear his head and settle his nerves if he could, and in spite of being tired, he thought a walk would do him some good.

Keeping away from the trail that had led them to so much trouble, he climbed the hill to the west. Downslope from the spot where the trail crested the ridge, he looked back to the east to see if he could get a glimpse of Fred. The trail had disappeared into the canyon, though, and all he saw was the land rising up bare on one side and wooded on the other.

Looking west, he could see once again where the country broadened into the little valley before it narrowed again at the last ridge. He could see the spot where Rusk and Marianne had set their camp, vacant now, and he could see the gap at the end of the valley. Beyond the gap, the country opened up onto the plains. He knew that somewhere out there was a place called Pass Creek, a station of some sort, and beyond that and a ways south was Warm Springs. He imagined Rusk and Marianne making their way out into the wide country, perhaps stopping in Warm Springs before going on their way for better or for worse.

Vance thought about Rusk going off in one direction and Fred in the other, and he was glad he was not either of those two men. One was bound to spend the rest of his life with a chip on his shoulder, always resentful that he didn't get his revenge, and the other would always have to wonder if there was someone coming up behind him. And a man who had taken another man's wife and killed the man for good measure would have himself to live with, no matter how stoic he was.

Vance looked at the valley below him. Somewhere down there, drops of blood would have fallen on leaves of sagebrush and blades of grass. Rusk would have gone out at dawn to see if anyone was lying in the brush, and he might have seen traces here and there, especially where Vance had found Tip lying down. Other than that, the area below, where Fred had been talked down to and Tip had gotten his fatal wound, was just another place in a big country. The shadow of a hawk would move over the sage and grass, the wind would ripple it, and the snow would cover it. The land would go on its own way, as it had done for ages, and no one would know the places where sharp words and fast bullets had flown.

Vance stood on the hill for several minutes, seeing the land stretch away paler and paler beyond the gap. Maybe some day he would ride out that way and see more of the country, but Rattlesnake Pass was as far as he was going to go on this trip.

He looked at the sun. Two hours was a long time, but he imagined Fred would not be able to travel as fast as Vance could travel alone, and he didn't want to catch him too soon.

Vance walked down the hill and checked on his horse, which he had unsaddled and put out to graze at first light. He led the horse to water and then back to its picket. Somewhat at odds about how to fill the time, he rolled out his bed in the shade of some young cottonwoods. With a sigh he lowered himself and stretched out flat on his back, with his hat tipped over his eyes and his hands folded on his stomach.

He awoke to the sound of cottonwood leaves rustling. Sitting up and looking around, he saw his horse at the end of the picket rope, as before. Squinting upward, he could see that the sun had moved, but not much.

Figuring he still had about an hour to kill, he went to the creek and washed his face, then decided to stretch his legs again. Something made him want to take another look at the country to the west, so he climbed the hill to the spot where he had stood earlier. Once there, he saw the same landscape as before, broad sweeps of paling country beneath an endless sky.

As he let his gaze rove, a slight movement just this side of the gap caught his eye. Watching, then relaxing his eyes and watching again, he saw what it was. Someone had come upcountry through the gap and was headed this way. For a moment he lost sight of the movement, then picked it up again. It was two riders. He doubted that it was Rusk and Marianne, but he imagined that whoever it was might have seen the other two.

He looked at the sun again as he stepped downhill to keep from skylining himself. He wondered if he should try to get out on the trail ahead of these travelers or if he should wait to get a look at them. He figured Fred had an hour's start on him, and even though he imagined they would end up traveling together, he didn't want to catch up with him the first morning. Depending on how fast these other fellows were moving, it might be just as well to let them go by, and then he could fall in a ways behind.

Going up the hill far enough to see over the crest, he picked out the two riders again. They were moving along pretty well. That would be all right. If the looks of them didn't worry him, he could let them ride by. They would probably pass up Fred before the day was halfway gone.

Vance settled down out of sight again, deciding to wait where he was until he got a good look at these other two travelers. As he crouched on the hillside, he could feel the warmth of the sun against the bare dirt and rocks, and he began to sweat. Standing up and seeing the riders not much closer than before, he decided to walk downhill, kill a few minutes, and walk back up again.

Down he went, conscious now of the faint jingle of his spurs. At the bottom he yawned and stretched, paced around, and looked after his horse. Then he climbed the hill again.

The two riders had come closer, almost to the spot where Rusk and Marianne had camped. They were loping across the flat, not wasting any time. It was two men, and their shapes looked familiar. Vance dropped out of sight for a couple of minutes and then took another look. He knew the two riders, all right — two buzzards who at the moment were not sitting on a fence rail. They were moving fast enough now that Vance realized he would not have time to saddle up and get out on the trail with any kind of a lead — not unless he wanted them to think he was running from them. And that was one of two things he wasn't doing. He wasn't chasing anyone and he wasn't running.

Chapter Fourteen

Winslow and Ludington seemed to know where he was, as they rode straight off the trail toward his camp. They drew rein a few yards away, and Ludington spoke.

"Where's Brother Dunham?"

"Not here."

"I can see that." The buggy eyes roved around, taking in the various parts of the campsite. "Looks like he pulled out. What about his little brother?"

"He's got Tip with him."

Ludington's eyes roved some more. "Uh-huh."

"What do you want him for?"

"I need to ask him a question." The button nose lifted. "But now that we're here, I could ask you one, too."

Vance waited a few seconds before answering and then said, "Go ahead."

Ludington twisted his face into half a smirk and looked at him askance. "What are you doing here by yourself?"

"Minding my own business." Vance did not like either of the men, especially

Ludington, and he didn't have it in him to feign friendship.

Ludington looked at Winslow and then back at Vance. "Well, aren't we smart? Why didn't you pull out with the others?"

"I thought I'd wait and then go along on my own."

"You're a long ways from home to be doin' that, aren't you?"

"I've got no quarrel with anyone, so I don't know why I should worry."

With both hands on the saddle horn, Ludington squared himself up. "Well, you travel with troublemakers, and people remember that."

"I'm traveling by myself."

"You weren't the other day, and one of your party was gravely injured, as they say."

"I didn't start that fight, and I didn't get into it."

"You were there."

"I was riding along with the Dunham brothers."

"We didn't like it."

Vance looked from Ludington to Winslow. He knew what they were capable of, but he also knew it wouldn't do to show that he was intimidated. "I didn't like it either," he said. "And unless your little snitch handed in his dinner pail, he came out of it better than Shorty did."

"We still didn't like it," Winslow piped up.

Vance turned and met the quick brown eyes trained on him. He wondered if Winslow and Ludington were passing him back and forth, working together at baiting him. "Look," he said. "Enough men have been hurt and killed in the past few days. Why don't we leave it at that?"

Winslow showed his yellow teeth. "Is that right? Well, let me tell you something. We've still got a bone to pick with the Dunhams and we don't need to take any guff from you in the meanwhile. Just remember, you're all by yourself and a long ways from home."

"Seems like a lot of people are."

Ludington gave his button-nose smirk. "Yeah, but most of 'em have sense to travel in company."

Vance had a hunch. "Oh, did you see the Mexican?"

"What Mexican?"

"I thought maybe your little snitch would have told you about him, and I believe Fred mentioned him the other day. I thought you might've gone to take a look at him yourself."

Ludington seemed to catch the drift. "Don't worry about what we've seen or haven't seen. Especially if you like to say you're mindin' your own business."

"Maybe I'll just go back to doin' it, then. It's what I was doin' before you came along."

"Might be the best thing for you."

Vance could tell that the two thugs, even though they had the time to stop by and be belligerent, weren't looking for trouble with him. He guessed that they had been trailing from a distance, maybe watching from the high points, and had gone around to catch up with Rusk. At least they were coming from that distance and looking for Fred, which could well mean that Rusk managed to brush them back in this direction. Whatever they had seen or heard, they seemed to know where the Dunhams had camped the night before, and they did not seem to know that Tip was dead. Vance felt guilty at pushing them off on Fred, but the sooner he got rid of them, the better he liked it.

"Fine," he said. "I don't think I've got anything else to say."

Ludington yanked back on his reins and made his horse turn its head and bare its teeth. At the same time, he brushed his right hand past the handle of his six-gun. "You might know how to stay out of trouble after all."

Vance said nothing as he watched the two men head their horses back onto the trail and put them into a lope. Once they were gone, he went back to his bed and sat on it, thinking, with his arms hooked around his knees. He had succeeded at getting rid of Winslow and Ludington, but he didn't feel good about what they might have in store for Fred. Vance thought they were using the fight from a few days earlier as a pretext for starting an argument, and he imagined their other motive could well have something to do with the money Moon swindled from them or their employers. Rusk might have said something clever enough to make them want to see what they might be able to squeeze from Fred. With two motives for harassing him, then, and with the discovery that he was not only on his own but handicapped with the body of his brother, they might give Fred quite a bit of trouble.

Vance stared off at the trail where Fred had left earlier and where the other two had followed. No matter how much he had come to dislike Fred's attitudes, he did not like the unfairness of Winslow and

Ludington bullying him when he was trying to transport his dead brother. And although Fred was a cad, he ranked higher on Vance's scale than the other two did. Whether they carried out their work undercover, as they were reported to have done with Nate Cousins and others, or whether they did it outright, as Ludington did with Shorty, they had no scruples.

Vance shook his head. He was weary of the whole business and had hoped to be shut of it, but he knew what he ought to do, so he pushed himself up onto his feet and started to pack his gear.

Within fifteen minutes he had his horse saddled and his bedroll and bag tied on behind. The horse, which had rested well, was ready to go, so Vance let him out at a brisk walk and within a few minutes nudged him into a lope.

The country flowed by — the same hills and trees and brush he had seen the day before, but scenes he was now leaving behind and did not need to study. Uphill and down, around curves and along straightaways, he rode eastward through Rattlesnake Pass. He could picture, strung out somewhere on the trail ahead, Winslow and Ludington trying to close in on the Dunham brothers. If they hadn't caught up already, they would do so soon enough.

Whatever they did to Fred, they would do it as he was trying to haul his brother home, and that seemed like an indignity. Vance felt as if, in a detached way, he were still looking after Tip, but he also knew that in spite of their differences, he was going to stick up for Fred.

On he rode, trying to keep a cool head but knowing he didn't have time to waste. He didn't push the horse, but he didn't hold it back, either, and it had plenty of energy after the bit of a rest it had gotten.

Then, in the deepest part of the pass, at the bottom of a grade where the landscape opened up a hundred yards on each side of the trail, he caught up with all of the others at once. Fred was lying bareheaded on the ground, his three horses had crowded together near the creek, and the two riders were sitting on their horses facing the trail that came from the west. From Fred's posture, Vance imagined that Winslow and Ludington had finished their piece of business with him. As a reflex, Vance checked to see that his six-gun was in place as he slowed his horse. Then he came in at a walk, holding the reins with his left hand as usual.

Ludington spoke first. "I thought you

were learnin' to mind your own business."

"I was." As Vance brought his horse to a halt, he saw Fred rise up on an elbow and turn his head to see who had ridden in.

"You would have done better to have stayed behind."

Vance met Ludington's gaze and saw the smirk again. "I thought I'd come and check on Fred."

"He'll be all right," said Winslow. "We just had to talk to him."

Vance, turning to see Winslow, looked farther to get a better view of Fred, and he saw what the talk had consisted of. Fred's face was swollen and bruised, with his left eye swelling shut, and his matted blond hair was powdered with dirt.

"Thing is," said Ludington, "we don't like to have our conversations inter-rupted."

"I see," said Vance, turning to his left to meet the bug eyes.

"You see," mimicked Ludington. "You see more than you need to." Then his voice took on more menace. "Git down from your horse."

Vance stayed in the saddle and relaxed his reins by an inch. His horse shifted weight and sidestepped.

"I said, git down," Ludington ordered.

Vance looked him in the eye. "I don't know what for."

"Maybe we want to talk to you, too." He motioned with his head toward Fred. "He begged us not to pull the trigger. Maybe you'll do the same."

Vance held his place and nudged his horse so that it continued to sidestep. "I've got no business with you, and you've got none with me."

Ludington lifted his chin and looked down his button nose. "I told you to git off that horse. I don't know which of these brothers you want to look like when we're done, but you can make it easier on yourself if you do what you're told. Now you keep your horse still and git down."

Out of the corner of his eye, Vance saw that Winslow had taken down his rope and was shaking out a loop. Looking back at Ludington, Vance found himself looking at the barrel of a .45. He thought that if he could keep the horse milling, he would make a harder target for the six-gun. The other two men's horses had begun to move, too, and as he wondered what their move was going to be, Winslow's horse stepped away in Fred's direction. Vance looked again at the bore of the six-gun leveled at him, and then to his right he saw

Winslow's rope in motion. The loop shot out and slapped around Fred's neck.

Winslow's horse shied and threw him off balance before he could wrap his dallies. As he brought the horse under control, Ludington spoke.

"If you care about what happens to your pal Fred, you'll git down now."

Vance saw that Winslow had dropped the coils, and now held the rope and his reins in his left hand as he tried to gather up the loose half of the rope with his right. In that instant he saw an opening, so he kicked his spurs into his horse and lunged forward. Winslow's horse jumped aside and the rope fell to the ground. Ludington's pistol roared as the bullet split the air but went wide.

Vance could see Ludington turning his horse to try to pick up the moving target, so he wheeled his own horse back around and let Ludington's line of fire pass him up. As Ludington tried to stop and regroup, Vance cut left. With his gun drawn, he bolted right past Winslow, whose horse was rearing. When he was in the open again, he heard a second shot rip past him, and then he heard the boom of the .45. Vance bent low over his horse's neck and heard two more shots whistle over.

Figuring he was out of range until the others either gave chase or pulled out rifles, he put his pistol away and cut right, crossing the trail on which he had ridden in. Then he felt his horse shudder and he heard the crash of a rifle.

The horse did not fall, but Vance knew it was hit. As he brought it to a stop near a clump of brush at the base of the hill, he felt the second shot slam into its body. He swung down to the off side, his left, and pulled out his rifle.

The horse was still standing, but it was hunched up and wheezing. As Vance levered in a shell and looked around the rump end of the horse, he could see Ludington kneeling some sixty yards away and bringing up his rifle for a steady shot. Vance lined up his sights and pulled the trigger, and Ludington snapped backwards to the ground, dropping the rifle where he had knelt.

Now for Winslow. Winslow's brown horse stood farther back than Ludington and still to the left of Fred. Vance could not place the man until he saw a pair of boots on the ground beneath the horse's front quarters. The rest of the man disappeared behind the body of the horse and the reins were pulled snug on the off side.

Winslow was using his horse as a shield, clear enough.

Vance knew he had better do something before his own horse keeled over, so he levered in another shell and fired at the dirt behind the brown horse's front feet. As the horse scrambled and stopped, Winslow's bare head appeared above the withers and then went out of sight. He had hung onto the reins well enough, and probably with one hand, as he would have a rifle in the other.

Squinting in the bright overhead sun, Vance could make out the man's boots again. Winslow was standing behind the tallest part of the horse, keeping his hatless head behind the animal's neck and jaws. Vance figured he could shoot the horse just as Ludington had shot his, but he didn't want to unless he had to, so he drew the finest aim he could at the two inches of boot visible to the side of the horse's front left hoof.

Everything happened at once. The rifle blasted and the barrel went up, closing off Vance's view for a second. As he levered in another shell and got a full look again, he saw the brown horse sashaying around as Winslow leveled his rifle.

Vance fired again, and Winslow sank

with his rifle in his hands. The brown horse bolted away, his hooves pounding the ground, but all else was silent.

Vance walked across the open ground to the spot where Fred had sprawled out flat in the thick of the gunfight. Fred had gotten Winslow's rope from around his neck, and it lay on the ground not far from him.

"Are you all right, Fred?"

The blond head lifted and the body moved, then contracted as Fred rose again to one elbow and turned his battered face toward Vance. "You should have stayed out of it," he said. "They were done with me."

"I didn't know that when I got here. I came as soon as I could once I knew they were headed after you."

"You didn't have to."

Vance felt like throwing his rifle on the ground, but he kept his hold on it. "I didn't have to do a damn thing," he said. "Not one damn thing, from the very beginning. But I did. I rode off with you two, and I came back to stick up for you."

Fred moved his head back and forth with a very slow motion. "You wouldn't do it when I asked you, and you did when I didn't need it. You could have got us both killed."

Vance recalled Ludington's comment about Fred begging not to be killed, and he wondered how much of it was true. "Maybe I shouldn't have bothered," he said, "but I knew what they could do. And I remembered what they did to Shorty."

"You remember what you want to. What about the son of a bitch that killed my two brothers?"

Vance let out a long breath. "We've already gone through all of that."

Fred shook his head again. "Not me. I'm not forgettin' a damn bit of any of this."

Vance caught a movement at the edge of his vision. Looking around, he saw his horse flopped on its side with a small cloud of dust rising around it. That was one more problem to get around, he thought. At least at the moment there wasn't a shortage of horses. Turning back to Fred, he said, "I know you don't want to forgive or forget a damn thing. But you can use my help gettin' back to Rock River." He held out his hand and helped Fred to his feet.

"Yeah, you can ride along. But I just wish to hell you would've helped me when I asked. That son of a bitch needed it worse than either of these two."

Vance held his tongue. It was going to be

a long ride back with someone who would never give up his bitterness, and who would never see that if he had given it up the evening before, it would have cost everyone a lot less. As for himself, he remembered why he had come on this trip — because of a stated belief that a man had a right to get even. But that whole idea had turned out to be a twisted one — kinks in the rope, as Shorty had said. And even if Vance had settled the score for Shorty, or anyone else at the same time, it did not bring him satisfaction. He would rather have let it all go if he could. Two days' ride from here, a wife and a child waited for him. He could put up with Fred in the meanwhile and not bother to answer or argue, for he knew in his heart that he had learned to forgive, and knowing it for himself was good enough for now.